ON THIN ICE

ALSO BY MICHAEL NORTHROP

Trapped

Plunked

Rotten

Surrounded by Sharks

Polaris

The TombQuest Series

ON THIN ICE

BY MICHAEL NORTHROP

Scholastic Press

NEW YORK

Library of Congress Cataloging-in-Publication Data
Names: Northrop, Michael, author.
Title: On thin ice / by Michael Northrop. Description: First edition. | New York: Scholastic
Press, 2019. | Summary: The way twelve-year-old Ked Eakins of Norton, Maine, sees it his life
has been stolen from him, piece by piece; first by kyphosis, a spinal abnormality which has
made him a social outcast at school and a target for the school bully, by his friends who have
recently abandoned him, by his mother who left for the West Coast taking the insurance which
might have saved him with her, and by his father who is a gambling addict who has lost the rent
money—but Ked is a builder, and using the school's Maker Space he intends to build his life
back, and maybe make a few real friends, and save his father while he is at it.
Identifiers: LCCN 2018046395 (print) | LCCN 2018053901 (ebook) |
ISBN 9780545495929 | ISBN 9780545495905 (hardcover)
Subjects: LCSH: Kyphosis—Juvenile fiction. | Fathers and sons—Juvenile fiction. | Compulsive
gamblers—Juvenile fiction. | Conduct of life—Juvenile fiction. | Bullying—Juvenile fiction. |
Interpersonal relations—Juvenile fiction. | Friendship—Juvenile fiction. | Maine—Juvenile
fiction. | CYAC: Kyphosis—Fiction. | Spine—Abnormalities—Fiction. | Fathers and
sons—Fiction. | Gambling—Fiction. | Conduct of life—Fiction. | Bullying—Fiction. |
Interpersonal relations—Fiction. | Friendship—Fiction. | Maine—Fiction.
Classification: LCC PZ7.N8185 (ebook) | LCC PZ7.N8185 On 2019 (print) |
DDC 813.6 [Fic]—dc23

10 9 8 7 6 5 4 3 2 1   19 20 21 22 23

Printed in the U.S.A.   23
First edition, August 2019

Book design by Keirsten Geise

"NOTHING MAKES A MAN SO ADVENTUROUS
AS AN EMPTY POCKET."
—VICTOR HUGO, *THE HUNCHBACK OF NOTRE-DAME*

TABLE FOR ONE

I HATE THIS CAFETERIA. It feels like the scene of a crime. It's a slow crime that has taken years—a theft, I guess. I'm not sure anyone else has noticed, and why would they? The only thing that's been stolen is my whole life, piece by piece.

It's Monday and I'm navigating my tray through the maze of kids, tables, and noise. I figure I'll sit with Danny, like usual. We're in seventh grade now, Danny and me and pretty much everyone else I know.

Sixth-through-eighth-grade classes are in a separate building, down the hill. Technically, that's Norton Middle School and this upper building is Norton Elementary, but the schools are kind of jumbled together. We still hike back up to "the kids' building" for the cafeteria, gym, library, and a few other things. And the little kids stampede down to our building for art and music and anything in the auditorium.

The point is, I've been making this slow walk between these same tables for most of my life. Ever since October, when Nephi started sitting with the other guys who are big into the maker space, it's just been Danny and me at lunch. We usually sit at the table in the back corner.

But when I get to the table in the corner, Danny isn't there. *That's weird,* I think, *I could've sworn I saw him ahead of me in the line for this so-called pizza.* I whip my head around. My shirt is stretched tight across my shoulders. (For reasons I'll explain in a minute.) I can feel the fabric start to ride up in the back as I give it a good neck tug from side to side. My eyes are suddenly wide open, alert, maybe a little panicky.

When I spot Danny, he's looking at me too. But he looks away fast. He's at a table full of people. I know that table. We tried to join it back in the fall, after Neff made his move. They didn't let us. "Nah, guys. Sorry. No space."

Now I understand: I was the problem.

I don't know why that surprises me. I don't know why any of this does. I'm always the problem these days. I guess I just expected a little more from Danny—a little more loyalty, a little more time. We've been eating together since that meant scarfing down Goldfish crackers on little rugs on the kindergarten floor. We were neighbors back then too. We went to opening day of fishing season together every year. One year he caught a trout as big as his forearm, and I was the one who netted it for him.

I get a sick, cold feeling. Danny knows I'm still here, but he's not acknowledging me. The other kids at his new table aren't

2

even that popular, I tell myself—but it's a full table, so how unpopular could they be?

And me? I'm standing here with my tray of chocolate milk, an apple, and a square pizza with the bite I took out of it back in line. I look down at the empty table in front of me. I can feel my heart beating faster. I've been coming to this cafeteria since I was in first grade, since it was just our heads and shoulders above the tabletops. Since I was one of the kids at the full tables.

The next table over has space, but just seeing me glance over, they close ranks, scooting their butts a little closer together on the curved benches attached to the flying saucer–shaped table. My hair is long in the front, almost to my eyes. I reach up with one hand and push it back.

I know that the longer I stand, the more I stand out. It feels like people are starting to stare. At me, at my back. I stand up as straight as I can, but it's pushing up and out against my shirts. I usually wear two: a T-shirt and an unbuttoned button-up. The button-up is a size too big for most of me, but that still makes it a size too small for my back. Every year, my back bulges out a little farther, pushing out against the fabric. That's what I imagine my classmates staring at now, stealing looks from behind me or off to the side. I hear laughter and my heart starts hammering.

Who's laughing? Why? It could just be some dumb joke or someone dropping their pizza cheese-side down. But when I look over at the table, I know it's not. The guys sitting there are like the kings of my grade. They're popular, athletic, and even smart. I

3

make eye contact with their leader, the human mountain Landrover Jones. He doesn't even bother to hide his smirk.

I drop my tray on the round, empty table in front of me. It clatters loudly. It doesn't matter. The volume in the cafeteria is at jet-engine level. Everyone is talking, everyone is joking. And anyone who was going to stare at me is already doing it.

I sit down alone. Everyone says we're never going to use most of what we learn in school. But some of it's important. Right now I'm thinking about math. I'm thinking about addition and subtraction all at once. I'm thinking about how everything you subtract adds up.

When Maps left our table last year, there were still three of us: Nephi, Danny, and me. We didn't even take it that personally. We all knew Maps was different. He was an instant star on the middle school teams. He had teammates to talk to and games to plan. And even when Nephi made his move to the makers' table, there was still Danny. There was still someone left. They were never leaving me alone. It was easier for me and, honestly, I think it was easier for them too.

They're not bad guys. At least I never used to think so. We all knew the deal: Things change. New classes, new teams, new schedules, and so yeah, sometimes that's going to add up to new friends and new tables. It was almost like a game of musical chairs: one less player each time. You just start up again with whoever is left.

But now Danny is gone. Subtract one, like every time before. But this time it leaves me with zero. Game over: not enough players.

Danny didn't do anything different than the others. He just did it last. He was my last friend from before, but now he has slipped away like a fish with no one to net it. I'm alone. It happened piece by piece and then all at once. Now, it's down to me and what's left of this sad, soggy piece of pizza. The table is big and round and white, like the beam of a spotlight. Like the number zero.

Welcome to the rest of my life, I think.

I hate this cafeteria.

And it hates me back.

SPIDER-MAN, THE HULK

MY NAME IS KED EAKINS, and I live in Norton, Maine. I think maybe I forgot to mention that up front. Anyway, everyone used to call me Ked. It's an unusual enough name that it was basically its own nickname. Now people have started to call me "Freakins"—or sometimes just "Freak."

For the record, I prefer Ked.

I wasn't always like this. I used to be just another kid. I don't know if you'd say popular, but I had friends, and we had fun. We did normal stuff. But things started to change a few years ago. I started to change. I remember the first time I noticed something unusual about my back. I'd just taken a bath. And, okay, fine: It was a bubble bath. I was still into Mr. Bubble back then.

Anyway, I was drying off and I felt something on my back. You know how your spine is basically a line of little bumps under your skin? Well, it kind of felt like one of my bumps had a brother, and that brother had started to wander up my back and press out against the skin a little more. And as weird as that sounds, I wasn't too worried about it at first. It just felt a little swollen or tight or something. But I'd just gotten out of the bath, my whole body was warm and relaxed—and I was just standing there naked anyway. I reached back over my shoulder and really got in there, and when I did: *Ouch!* It was kind of tender.

I wiped the last of the steam off the mirror with my *Star Wars* towel. What was going on back there? I twisted my neck all the way around to look at myself. I still remember that moment so well. Me standing there looking super scrawny with my butt so much paler than the rest of me. But I still couldn't decide if it was a real, visible lump on my back.

I remember thinking that maybe it was a spider bite. Or not a spider bite exactly. What I am about to say is deeply stupid, but remember, I was younger then. And dumber. So what I really thought was that maybe a spider had injected its eggs into me and pretty soon they would hatch and all these little baby spiders would erupt from my skin. I'd heard a story at sleepaway camp where that happened. It was just a dumb story the counselors told to scare us, but it's the first thing I thought. I was scared. And the amazing thing about it is that, looking back now, I wish it *had been* spider eggs. Heck, tarantulas would be okay with me. At least it would all be over by now. I'd have a cool scar and a *great* story for camp!

It's almost funny, but the other thing I remember isn't funny at all. When I looked back as much as I could, when I really hoot-owled my head around, the skin on my upper back felt tight. It just refused to stretch anymore, like it was stuck.

That was the first time I felt that, and it just got worse from there. Now I can't even really look back over my shoulder on the left side. Which is just as well. I wouldn't like what I saw.

But I'm getting ahead of myself. Back then I pulled on my underwear—goodbye, pale butt!—and my pants too. That was in case I had to be rushed to the hospital, or maybe to the veterinarian because of the spiders. I wasn't sure. I left my shirt off. Then I took a big, deep breath. The air was warm and still smelled like Mr. Bubble. Without bothering to open the door, I yelled, "MOM!"

She came in fast. She always paid extra attention when I was in the bath, even though I wasn't a baby anymore. I showed her the suspected bump and explained to her, as calmly as I could manage, that she was about to be a grandmother to five hundred or possibly a thousand spiders.

She assured me that she was not. That made me feel better and I was ready to forget the whole thing. But then she started poking the little tight spot too. I was like: "Ow!" Then she took her hand and began running it up and down my spine, from below my shoulders all the way up to my neck. She'd already been on me about my posture for a while by then, always telling me to "stop slouching," so I did my best to stand up straight. Her palm felt soft and warm.

"What?" I said.

"Nothing," she said. "Everyone's spine curves a little."

Yeah, I told myself. *Totally normal.*

But she decided that I should go to the doctor after all. There was no insect-eruption urgency. She just wanted to get it checked out. She made an appointment for later in the week.

We did things like that back then: Trips to the doctor just to check things out, regular checkups at the dentist. My mom had a good job, which meant good insurance and decent money too—at least when my dad wasn't blowing it all.

We went to the hospital on Friday afternoon. I wasn't worried at all. I was psyched—like, *Maybe we'll get ice cream after?* At that point, I had never had anything wrong with me that required more than some Pepto-Bismol or a Band-Aid. But once I got to the hospital, things started to change. The doctor made me get X-rays of my back. I pretended the radiation was going to turn me into the Incredible Hulk.

He studied the X-rays for a long time without saying anything. So did my mom. They were right up on the wall, and I could've looked too if I wanted. But I didn't. I told myself it was because they were gross—*Those are my bones!* But that wasn't really it. I sat there looking at my feet and remembering how it felt when my mom ran her hand over my back.

Then the doctor did the same thing! His hand felt rough and cold. After that, he had me do a bunch of stretching and reaching, like I was trying out for a gymnastics team or something. Some of it hurt a little. Then I got to put my shirt back on and they sent me home with a "We'll be in touch." It sounded serious.

I had to lean forward away from the car seat as Mom drove us home. I can't even remember if we got ice cream.

The verdict came in the next week. I remember my mom sitting there and explaining it all to me. My dad was there too, so I knew it was serious. I saw my dad less than my mom back then, and I was a lot less close to him. He was "the enforcer," because he's big and quiet most of the time, so it's scary when he yells. Mom was always like: "Don't make me tell your father!" It was a weird thing to say, though, because most of the time he was in more trouble than me. He was always losing money on stupid bets. It was like he couldn't help himself.

But he's the one who stuck around, so I guess you never know. Now the guy who couldn't help himself has to help us both. Mom moved to Portland, and not Portland, Maine, either. She lives in the other one, the fun one they set TV shows in. Sometimes I like to think she's having a great time out there in Oregon. Sometimes I like to think she's not.

She did all the talking that day. I remember words like "spinal abnormality" and "adjacent vertebrae." My spine was starting to curve forward—"excessive rounding"—like a bend in a river.

It's called kyphosis. (There's another name for it, but I don't use that word.) It mostly happens to old people, when their spine is breaking down, but it can happen to kids too, when their spine is growing. The vertebrae just start growing unevenly. They should be rectangles, but some of them become more like wedges, and the whole spinal tower starts to lean.

Then Mom said something important. She said I'd have to wait until I stopped growing before we could "even think about operating," which, I mean, I hadn't been. Not till then.

I just sat there and listened. I thought of the little pains I felt sometimes, reaching up to the cupboard for the cereal or rolling over in bed at night. That's when I realized: That wasn't normal. That wasn't something everyone felt. My head was buzzing from all the new information. When Mom stopped talking she looked down at the papers in front of her and we were all quiet for a little while. Finally I said, "But then they can fix it, right? After I stop growing?"

Dad and I looked at her.

"They think there's a good chance," she said. She reached up and wiped the corner of one eye. *Was she crying?* Then she took a deep breath, forced a smile for like a second, and kept going. She talked about "surgical options" or "fusing the spine." I wasn't too excited about any of that, obviously.

She said my condition was developing early and fast, and they'd just have to wait and see. In the meantime, they thought a back brace might help. I groaned. "It all depends on how things develop," she said for like the third time. And she didn't say it, but it would depend on something else too. It would depend on keeping that good insurance.

It was one of those days when your whole life changes in an instant, like the day Bruce Wayne's parents are killed. The difference is, I didn't know it yet. My mom was saying they would have to wait until "after adolescence" at least. And I was sitting there thinking, *What's the big deal? Why do you two look so sad?*

Because I was thinking, *It's so small.* I was thinking, *I didn't even notice it until I took that bath.* I knew it would keep bending and bulging out—maybe all the way through adolescence. I just didn't realize it would get so serious. It had taken *my whole life* just to get to the point where I noticed it. I thought it would keep going at that same pace. Even if I was twice as old when it stopped, that was just double. I was imagining another few degrees around the river bend, a lump like half a lemon.

I wasn't being stupid, exactly. I just had the time frame wrong. My body was just starting to think about adolescence, but my condition was already off and running.

And no one told me either. Maybe Mom was hoping it wouldn't be so bad. Maybe she didn't want to get ahead of herself. Maybe she was researching possibilities online. I still don't know. But I do know that she left, and I know that she took that good insurance with her.

After that Dad and I got something called "catastrophic coverage." Basically, it will cover us if we get hit by a bus. Short of that, we're on our own. The doctors got a lot more blunt after that, or maybe just more honest. I remember waiting forever to see our new doctor. He was really young for a doctor. When he finally came in the room, he looked at my dad and said we'd have to let my condition "run its course."

"Like a forest fire?" I asked, but he didn't answer me. He barely even looked at me. I should've asked: "Isn't this catastrophic?" I bet he would've looked at me then.

I don't want to talk about that now, though.

What I want to talk about is that pale butt in the mirror.

THE LAKE

THE REASON MY BUTT was so much paler than the rest of me was because I used to go to the lake a lot in the summer. The lake is probably the nicest thing about my town.

People call Norton "a failing mill town." It has a lot of broken-down houses and rusty cars and empty stores with signs in the windows that say "Commercial Space Available," and it has a big old factory right on the river. They used to make paper in that huge brick building, and then they used to make shoes. Now it's half empty. It's cheaper to make shoes somewhere else, so they just make the "leather uppers" for those cheap shoes here. And my dad works half the hours he used to, for half the pay.

That's what they mean by "a failing mill town." Jobs leave, people leave; no one new wants to move in. The town gets hollowed out, and the people who are left get bored and desperate and do dumb things. Dad complains about it a lot—then he turns around and does something dumb himself. But Norton has been failing for my whole life, so it's taking its time about it. And in the meantime, it has a really nice lake.

That first summer, after I found out, I still went to the lake all the time with my friends. With Danny, Nephi, and especially Maps. His real name is Tom Mapplewitz, and he was my best friend by then. Even though Danny lived closer and I'd known him longer, Maps was my best friend for pretty much as long as I'd known him. We were like brothers. We liked all the same video games and comic books and corny jokes. We liked all the same sports too, even though Maps was always better at actually playing them than I was. Maps was better at playing them than *everyone* was.

Anyway, we would swim out to the big raft, where the little kids aren't allowed. It was the first summer we could go out there, and we were proud of it. Plus it had a high dive, and even if it wasn't all that high, it was something to do. We'd sit on the edge of the raft and talk and just kind of marvel at how far from shore we were. Then every once in a while someone would do a cannonball or a jackknife or dive straight down and try to swim all the way to the bottom of the lake. The deal with that was you had to come up with some seaweed or no one would believe you.

One day, toward the end of summer, we were sitting out there and talking about school. We couldn't believe that summer vacation was almost over.

"Fifth grade . . ." said Nephi. "Just when I was starting to figure out fourth."

I chuckled. Fourth grade had been pretty good by the end, but now: new teachers, new rules, middle school looming. We all stared down into the water and tried to imagine what it would be like. We weren't afraid or anything. We would be the oldest students in the upper building. We just didn't know what it had in store for us.

Danny, who'd known me longest, kept looking over at me. I knew something was on his mind. Finally he just went ahead and said it: "Dude man, what's up with your back?"

Maps shot him a look. Maps was our leader. He was already taller than the rest of us. His legs stuck farther down into the lake when we sat on the edge of the raft. It would be a long time before I understood the look Maps shot Danny that day.

I was still deep in denial then. I refused to believe that my back was really that different. It took a little more effort, maybe, but I could still stand up pretty straight. And okay, the lump was a little bigger, but not much. I told myself that the fact it had taken the others so long to notice was proof of how little I'd changed. But of course it hadn't taken them that long to notice. It had just taken that long for one of them to say something.

"It's nothing," I said. And because they were my friends, they let it go at that.

And then we were back to school. The days of hanging out in swim trunks were over. Fall starts early and winter lasts a long time in Maine, and you better believe you are fully clothed for both of them.

But fifth grade was the year things changed. I was in the

bathroom at home again. The mirror was even steamier because I'd finally given up on Mr. Bubble and started taking showers. I wiped the mirror with my towel and took a good long look. I couldn't pretend any longer. The first thing I noticed wasn't even the lump, even though that was growing. It was how much I was bent over, leaning forward. I tried to straighten up all the way, but I couldn't get there. I ran my own hand over the curve of my spine, as far back as I could reach. I remember thinking: *This is my new normal.*

I called my mom again and this time, standing there in all that Ivory soap smell, she came clean. "It's a progressive condition," she said. "Progressive" sounds like it should be good—*progress!* But she meant the opposite of that.

I finally understood. This change wouldn't be slow or small. My spine was curving in more, and it was happening faster. My spine was going to bulge out more and more. I felt the tears welling up in my eyes and I knew that I could either start bawling or start shouting. So I yelled at my mom for lying to me, for not telling me more the first time.

By that next summer, the lake was out of the question. I told my friends that I "wasn't into" swimming anymore. That I was thinking about taking up running instead. It was a total bluff. The little pinching pains had gotten worse by then. Even just standing up for too long was starting to cause a dull throbbing in my back.

I did go back to the lake once. My mom—still around, but just barely—had some errands to run nearby. I tagged along and wandered over to the lake while she was getting a haircut.

I stood there on the shore wearing an unbuttoned dress shirt loosely over my Avengers T-shirt, I had my new brace on underneath that. It was a good one, as light as they come. You could barely see it, but I was still sweating like a maniac under all those layers. I could see them out there on the big raft: Danny, Nephi, and Maps. Everyone except me. When I went back to the hair salon, Mom's hair was shorter than mine.

I snuck down to the lake again toward the end of the summer. It was just Danny and Nephi, no Maps. He was hanging out with them less and less. I think I was kind of the glue there, to be honest. I'm not bragging about that, because he was hanging out with me less too. He went to baseball camp and then to soccer camp. That was the story, anyway. I mean, it was true, but it was still an excuse. The real truth is that he had new friends: baseball friends, soccer friends.

So when I was finally ready to say something, I had to say it twice. First to the others and then to Maps. Both times, I admitted that something was "going on" with my back. "It's just a phase," I told them, which was kind of true. "Totally temporary," I added, which was less true. They all nodded very seriously.

"That's cool, man," said Nephi, even though it wasn't. "I was wondering."

Danny just shrugged and said, "I figured it was something like that."

Maps nodded too, when it was his turn, but he didn't say

anything at all at first. So with him I had to keep talking. He kept nodding, but that wasn't enough. Suddenly I needed to hear him say something. We both knew the deal. He was my best friend. I didn't know if I was still his, but he was still mine. Either way, I'd been keeping something big from him, something big and getting bigger. Finally, I blurted out the name of the condition.

He cut me off. "I *know*," he said. "I looked it up."

If you look up my name online, you can find the name of my condition. It's that rare. I'm medical famous. I just stared at him. I wondered how long he'd known. I wondered why it had taken me so long to tell him.

Sixth grade was when the train really started to go off the tracks. Part of it just happened to me, and part of it I did myself. First of all, I kicked off the year with my brief, unfortunate Hawaiian shirt phase. It was like making lemonade out of lemons, or that's what I told myself. Like: *Look how fun this extra shirt is!* But the shirts weren't fun—they were ugly and tent-like. It was like my upper half was going on a big, tacky campout.

We went from being the oldest kids in the upper building at school to being the youngest ones in the lower building. But more than that, we went from being a "we" to being a bunch of "mes" and an occasional "us." Maps made it a few months before he abandoned us at lunch. That's how it started. A month later, I was the only one he was still hanging out with.

Then word got out about my back, not just that there was "something going on" but also exactly what it was. I still refuse to believe that Maps is the one who told. We gave each other dumb, cheap Christmas presents as usual. I got him some graphic novels from the library sale, he got me a Batman key chain, and that was that. They were like parting gifts. He wasn't my best friend anymore after that. By February, he was officially one of the cool kids, I was officially one of the uncool kids, and we'd pretty much stopped talking. No one was surprised. It was just the next logical step for each of us. It was like evolution.

My mom pulled pretty much the same thing, but she dialed it way up. She showered me with Christmas presents. She spent big on my dad too.

"This is too much," he said, sitting on the floor in his red Christmas pajamas and looking down at his new guitar. They'd already started keeping their money separate. I knew that much from the arguments. They did it because Dad had a problem: gambling. With separate accounts, he couldn't lose all our money—just all of his. "How much did you spend?" he asked.

Mom just smiled at him. If I hadn't been breaking in my brand-new Xbox, I probably would have noticed how hard she was trying not to cry. She was in Oregon by New Year's. Dad and I watched the ball drop alone. I was wishing I could be playing my Xbox the whole time. He was probably wishing he could be playing his guitar.

That was the end of the Hawaiian shirts. We were down to whatever money Dad made and maybe the occasional check from Mom. Maybe from Granddad too. Dad never really says where the money comes from these days, but I know there isn't much of it.

That was the end of the brace too. The old one wasn't work-ing. The problem is in my upper back, and I needed a different kind. The picture of the cheap-o one Dad showed me was pretty bad. It had all these straps and a metal band that went around your neck.

He said I'd have to wear it "up to twenty-three hours a day," and even then he couldn't promise it would make much of a difference. I heard him out, but I was like, "I am not wearing that." Honestly, he seemed relieved. I don't think he could really afford it.

Even good regular clothes are a stretch. We both get ours on the big seasonal sale days at the factory outlet stores. That way we get an extra markdown on already-marked-down clothes that were cheap to begin with. But they're "name brand." Dad always reminds me of that. He's not buying me junk.

I usually smile and say, "I really like this one!" or whatever, because at least he's still trying.

Dad buys my shirts extra big now. I think I said that already. He'll hold a shirt up in front of me and size it up like it's the shoe leather and I'm the shape he needs to cut it into. I'll look at it later and see that it's extra large.

"You'll grow into it," he'll say.

I nod, and what I think but don't say is: *Part of me will.*

DOWNHILL FAST

ALL RIGHT, WELL, I hope you enjoyed that little walk down memory lane. I know I didn't. Lunch is over now, and it's time to walk back down the hill to the middle school. It's the first week of March, but it's not that cold by Maine standards. Lately it's been climbing above freezing during the day and then slipping back below it at night. Pretty much none of the boys are wearing coats. It's a short walk and it's considered super uncool to wear a winter coat up the hill on the first halfway warm days of the year.

Danny is still talking to two of the guys from his new table. I'm too embarrassed to interrupt, so I just kind of trail behind them as we head out. He's not looking back, but he's got to know I'm here.

They make us line up once we get to the doors. Honestly, it's kind of a relief. I just line up where I am, behind two random girls named Haley and Becca.

We march through the double doors like soldiers going off to war, or at least that's what I pretend. The day is blustery and bright. The late-winter wind is whipping my face, and I squint into the light like I am a hard man about to make enormous sacrifices for his country.

This lasts like two seconds because I am wearing really loose clothes, as usual: a Yoda T-shirt with an unbuttoned shirt over it, plus cargo pants to balance out all the bagginess up top. Anyway, halfway across the parking lot a gust of wind hits me just right. It catches my clothing and suddenly I balloon up like the sail of a ship. Anchors aweigh, boys!

My oversized white button-up is flapping around me. My T-shirt is inflating into a big bubble, Yoda expanding like a puffer fish.

"Holy cow," whoops a boy named Gino. "Freakins is gonna take off!"

They're laughing, but I can't see them. I'm struggling to pin my shirt down with one hand and button it with the other. Everything is flapping and moving. I'm leaning forward, head down. And then: BAM! My forehead crashes into something.

I look up. *Oh no.* It's Haley. She must have turned around to see what was happening, and I ran into her. I basically head-butted her.

More laughter busts out up and down the line. Mrs. Gallego yells at everyone to quiet down and then rushes over to see if Haley is okay. She's holding her nose, and I'm going, "Sorry sorry

sorry sorry" and still trying to button the last few buttons. The laughter turns to excited chatter. I get the last button buttoned and look around.

Danny looks away fast, but it's too late. I saw him. He wasn't smiling or joking like everyone else, but to me, his expression was a million times worse. It was relief. He decided to ditch me at lunch, and what did I do? I proved him right.

Things quiet down and it feels like maybe this will blow over. But then I hear a single voice, loud and deep. "Freak broke her nose!"

"Landrover!" shouts Mrs. Gallego. He's not really in trouble, though. He's a total golden boy. The teachers just draw the line at "Freak."

"Sorry," he says, but he's not really sorry either. I know because he's smiling his big, perfect smile.

Landrover Jones is named after a truck and built like one. He's huge, and he's given me trouble for years. It started when I was Maps's best friend and he was Maps's biggest rival for best athlete, but it's gotten worse lately. He pushed me to the ground right before Thanksgiving. He said I bumped into him. I stayed down and didn't argue. I avoid him as much as possible.

"It's broken," I hear. "He totally broke it."

I didn't! I would have heard it or felt it or something, right? But all I manage to do is shake my head and go, "Nuh-uh!"

Becca slaps me on the back and says, "Jerk! Look where you're going."

I clench up and suck in air through my teeth. It hurts when people hit me there.

"Becca! That's enough!" yells Mrs. Gallego, and everyone knows Becca won't get in trouble either, even though she hit me.

"I'm really sorry," I say to Haley.

She takes her hands away from her nose. No blood. Not bent. I relax a little.

"Everyone back in line!" Mrs. Gallego shouts.

Haley turns back around without a word and everyone else falls into formation. I can hear the talk all around me as we march down the hill. People will be picking over the bones of this for the rest of the day, at least.

Then, from way at the front, I catch a glimpse of Maps, a full head higher than everyone around him, looking back over his shoulder at me. He gives me an in-between look, not a smile and not a frown. I'm not sure what it means, but I know it's not relief.

He didn't want this. None of us did. It's just middle school. It's rough.

I don't want to make this seem worse than it is. Most of the time, my classmates are fine to me. Sometimes they're even nice. We've all been told to "choose kind" a million times by now. There's this one girl named Allie who used to come up to me every week and say, "Hi, Ked. How are you feeling?" And the way she said "feeling" had a few extra *e*'s in it. Then she'd listen to my answer, blink a few times, and say, "That's good" or "That's too bad" and walk away.

Other kids are more normal about it. They'll complain about a test, ask me about homework, even joke around—as long as it's more or less one-on-one. As long as they don't have to go on the record as actually liking me. As long as I don't try to sit at their table at lunch.

One day, about a month ago, I walked up to Allie. I don't know why. Danny was out sick, and I guess maybe I was feeling kind of alone. Anyway, she was with her friends, and they all got really quiet when I walked over. I pretended not to notice and was just like, "Hey, Allie. What's up?"

She looked horrified. She turned bright red and mumbled, "Not much." And those were the last two words she said to me. She hasn't asked me how I'm *feeeeeling* since. It's like we had an agreement and I broke it.

It kind of feels that way with my old friends too. They'll still smile at me in the hallway sometimes, still nod as we pass. They just won't stop. I've seen it so many times by now that I already know how it's going to go with Danny. I'm being blown off.

I know they'd disagree. They'd say we just have different friends now. They'd say that things change. And I'd say, *By "things," do you mean my back?* But even as I think it, I know that's not fair. They're not the ones who stare at me or make fun of me or call me Freak. They've never done any of that. But they've seen other kids do it. And unlike me, they can opt out.

COLD SPAGHETTI

WE LIVE IN AN APARTMENT IN TOWN NOW, and it's close enough to walk. It's the second floor of a small house, so we have to take off our shoes as soon as we get in. I usually just hang out at home after school. I don't mind being alone. I've still got the Xbox.

I slow down as I approach my block, even though the wind is still whipping pretty good. By the time I reach the big oak at the edge of our yard, I'm moving like a snail going uphill. I scan the yard and lean forward to see down to the end of the driveway. I'm looking for one red car in particular or a man in a suit.

We're behind on the rent again. Dad says summer will be better because he can pick up extra work on the coast. He's waiting for the tourists the way bears wait for salmon. But that's still months away. "If you run into Mr. K, tell him I mailed it but forgot the stamp," Dad told me last week. That's a dumb excuse, though, and I don't like to lie to our landlord. I don't like the way he looks at me when I do.

But the coast is clear today. No red car, no dark suit. I speed up and cut across the yard toward our door. Once I'm inside, I know I'll have a few hours to myself. Dad usually gets home between five and six at night. He works the afternoon shift now because, like I said, the factory cut the shifts in half. Any more than that and they'd have to give him benefits. But one benefit he gets is sleeping late. He's almost always still asleep when I leave for school. If I'm in a bad mood, I slam the door.

But he's in charge when he's awake. I have to get off the Xbox as soon as he gets home. The first thing he does is turn on the TV, and anyway, he hates "the robots." That's who he blames for his shift getting cut in half. I used to argue. I was like, "Dad, I'm pretty sure Sonic the Hedgehog doesn't make leather uppers for shoes." But you can't reason with him about job stuff. Plus, I think his definition of "robot" is broad enough to include the Xbox. It's kind of true too, because it has taken over half his parenting shift.

He knows it, because he does a good job of picking up used games for cheap. He's like: "Is this one cool? It was only two bucks."

Usually if a game is only two bucks there's a reason, but I just say "Yeah" and go back to *Sonic* or *Battlefront II* or *Minecraft*, all of which Mom got me for full price before she left. They're a little old but still good games.

As soon as Dad gets home I head to my room, like usual.

"Is your homework done?" he calls from the couch.

"Doing it now!" I shout through my door.

I hear the *SportsCenter* theme and settle back in to a Gordon Korman book I got from the library. I read a lot.

We have spaghetti for dinner. Dad leaves the jar of store-brand sauce out on the table so we can pour more on if we want. It's made with "real meat flavoring" and I actually prefer it to the fancier stuff we used to have. I miss having a salad first, though. I used to like the bacon bits.

We have dinner at the small kitchen table. "Family time," Dad says. "Nonnegotiable." Often neither of us has anything to say. Today, though, I have a few things on my mind. I want to talk about Danny ditching me and about sitting alone. But I don't want Dad to worry about me or think I'm a loser. He's got enough to worry about.

"I ran into this girl today," I say instead. That seems easier. His mouth is full, but he looks up and raises an eyebrow to let me know he's listening. "Like, literally ran into her—with my head."

Dad swallows his spaghetti and says: "Sounds like she should look where she's going."

"Dad," I say. "*I* ran into *her.*"

He reaches for the sauce. "Well, then she should look where *you're* going."

I snort and a speck of pasta flies out of my mouth. That's the thing about my dad. He messes up more than almost anyone I know, but he is always on my side. Sometimes he's even funny.

After dinner, I get up to scrape off my plate into the trash. I press the trash can lever with my foot and the lid pops open. There, right on top, is a folded-up string of scratch-off lottery tickets. "Win For Life!" the top one promises.

"How'd you do?" I say, even though winners don't go in the trash.

He's still eating, but he looks over and sees where I'm looking. "Pretty good," he says. "Almost won a hundred thousand."

"Almost won" is how Dad says "lost." The one good thing about us being broke is that it keeps him from gambling as much. He still blows through a lot of scratch-off tickets, though. He says they don't count, but I don't see why not. I've seen him win $2 and $5 more times than I can count, and then just blow it on more tickets. If he starts thinking about anything bigger than the lottery, he's supposed to go to a meeting over at the Catholic church. "Our Lady of the Horse Track," he calls it. He never goes, though. He says he doesn't need to—and anyway, Mom's not here to make him.

I scrape the rest of my dinner onto his loser tickets. That's the thing about gambling: There are always more losers than winners. Sometimes it feels like my dad is the last person in the world to figure that out. And he was always the worst kind of gambler: superstitious. Lucky numbers, birthdays . . . a million dumb ways to lose.

I finish reading my book after dinner and look out my window to check the weather. It looks clear. A gust of wind rattles the windowpane, but I don't mind the cold much.

I sit on the edge of my bed and put on my boots. Then I grab my big green heavy-duty parka and my old backpack and head out into the living room.

"I'm going out," I say to Dad.

He peels his eyes off the TV just long enough to check the time on his phone. It's just a little after nine. He nods. "Don't turn left," he says, as usual. "And stay on the sidewalk." There's a pause as he mentally runs through his parenting checklist. "And don't be gone too long, or I'll come get you," he adds. I'm pretty sure he's bluffing.

"Okay," I say, pocketing the keys and zipping up my parka.

Our apartment has its own stairway. I throw open the door at the bottom and the cold wind slaps me in the face. It's a lot colder than it was during the day. My eyes water as I flip up my hood. It has a fake fur lining, so now I am looking out at the world through a little tunnel of fuzz.

I check our mailbox alongside the door because sometimes Dad forgets. It's empty, but it's not like I was expecting anything special. The Jibrils' mailbox is right next to ours. The Jibrils are from Somalia. Mr. Jibril came here for a factory job like five years ago, just like Nephi's dad—and then his shift got cut in half just like everyone else's. It was a pretty cruel trick, if you ask me.

He works the morning shift now, so he gets home right after my dad leaves. They must pass each other on the road sometimes, two men splitting one house and one job.

I head down the walkway, but halfway to the sidewalk I veer off. There's still some snow on the yard, and I want to feel it crunch under my boots. It's been extra crunchy lately because it melts a little more in the sun each day and then refreezes at night. Soon all this snow will be gone.

Nothing nice sticks around for too long around here.

THIN ICE DAYS

DAD ALWAYS TELLS ME TO TURN RIGHT. Left takes you to the edge of town. It takes you to boarded-up houses that are maybe abandoned but maybe not. To rusted-out cars and broken snowmobiles and junkyard dogs, outside in the cold with their ribs showing and ragged worn-out barks. To the left there are people with worse addictions than gambling.

To the right is downtown; to the right is the river. Our downtown isn't much compared to most towns', I guess, but our river is just as wet as anyone's.

I turn right and start walking. A few minutes later I pass our car. Dad's been parking it down the street so our landlord won't know when he's home. He's got a lot of tricks like that.

The sky is clear and there's lots of moonlight. The houses are closer together once I get downtown. A lot of old-timers live around here. Dad grew up in this town, and he knows most of their names. I can see a few windows glowing gold up and down the street, perfect boxes of light in the darkness. *There's a life behind each one*, I think, *an old person inside remembering stuff.*

I hear a car. A battered Subaru is coming my way. Its headlights hit me full on and light me up. I duck my head so the top of my hood shields my eyes. The car passes, and whoever's in there has no idea who I am. Everyone leans forward into the wind. Everyone looks lumpy and awkward in a parka.

Norton's downtown doesn't fit it anymore. It hangs loose like a too-big suit. I pass an empty lot with just the outline of a building left. I think it used to be a bank. The next building is still standing but half-empty. The lights on the second floor never come on anymore.

There's a lot of that down here: a lot of empty space, a lot of "For Rent" signs. I look across Main Street. One three-story building is nothing but a hair place now. They don't really need three floors for that, but there's nothing else to put inside. Dad says it used to be a store that sold everything—clothes, sporting goods, toys—like our own little department store. Now there's just one department: hair.

Another car whooshes past, going about seventy in a twenty-five zone. People around here are always in a huge hurry to go nowhere.

This all probably sounds pretty sad, but there are things I love about this town too. Like the way it's mostly quiet but there's just enough noise to let you know people are still doing their thing. If you hear a door slam and then the sound of heavy boots running, you know someone's late and it might snow later. And if you hear a car horn honk, it's usually just once, because there's never much traffic around here.

I duck down the alleyway behind Royston's Good Food Emporium, which is kind of like our supermarket, and a few other stores. I swing my old pack off my back and start going through the trash barrels for bottles and cans. Sometimes there aren't any because someone else beat me to it. But tonight I'm in luck: almost a buck. I do this at night because I would die a hundred deaths if anyone from school saw me. Once I have enough, I return the bottles and cans to the machines in front of the store. It's nice to have some spending money, even if it's just a little. And anyway, it's not so bad. I almost never dig down all the way to the bottom, where it can get kind of juicy.

The bottles and cans clink as I swing my pack back on and bend down to rub my hands clean on a patch of snow. And then I'm back out on the sidewalk. Just past the library there's a little snow-covered park. I see the river sliding by in the moonlight beyond the park and hear the water rustle and clink.

I turn into the park and head toward the pond at the far end. The concrete path glows gray in the moonlight, and black cracks slither in every direction. I imagine all the cracks are snakes and the river's noise is their hissing.

The pond is about as big as a hockey rink, and in midwinter, people use it for one. It's still frozen solid. There's no churning current to break up the ice here.

Smack-dab in the middle of the iced-over pond is a wooden tower. It's about twelve feet tall, and I'm pretty sure it used to be a lifeguard chair at the lake. It's painted blue and white now and there's a sign on top that says "Thin Ice Days, March 18–19! VFD Fund-raiser! Get Your Tickets!" Ticket sales are over now, but they messed up and made it all part of one sign, so that phantom sales pitch for the volunteer fire department will be up until the tower falls. That kind of thing is pretty typical around here.

A thick white rope runs from the tower to what looks like an old-fashioned gas streetlight on shore, but instead of a flickering flame on top, there's a big, round clock. The rope is stretched tight to a metal ring on the side of the clock.

Spring is coming, and it's almost time for Thin Ice Days. A lot of towns in Maine have these festivals. They're about lobsters or blueberries or things like that. Ours is about thin ice. I don't think they meant it that way, but it's pretty perfect. Thin Ice Days is one weekend a year, but this town is on thin ice the other 363 days too.

There's a parade, a concert, and other stuff like that. There's also the VFD fund-raiser. You pay three bucks and put down the date and time when you think the tower will fall. Someday soon, when the ice on this pond breaks up, the tower will fall into the water, and the rope will pull that ring right out. The clock will stop. Whoever comes closest to the right day and time will win five hundred bucks. The rest goes to the fire department.

I size up the scene, estimating how thin the ice has gotten. How much longer will the tower be standing? I purse my lips and push a plume of frosty breath out in front of me. It's a sucker's bet, but I had to buy one ticket. Everybody talks about it. *When's the ice gonna break? When's the tower gonna fall?* Plus, five hundred bucks—can you even imagine? I could finally get some new games and a better controller. Maybe some less junky clothes and some decent sneakers too.

My ticket's for St. Patrick's Day: Friday, March 17, at nine p.m. The time slots are every fifteen minutes during prime ice-melting time, but you can't go over. If it's after nine, I lose. Today's the sixth, so that's almost two weeks away. I got the date from *The Farmer's Year Booke.* It's this old-timey book with long-range weather forecasts and planting charts and gardening stories that Mom used to buy every year. I figured they must know some-thing if they've been around so long.

Anyway, this year the theme of Thin Ice Days is "Building a Better Norton." So in addition to the tower and concert and stuff, which we have every year, there's also a model-building competition for kids, a volunteer day to pick up trash in the park, and things like that.

My face feels warm and damp from my breath inside my hood. I lower the hood and let the chilly wind cool me down. I've been on my feet for a while now, and I can feel a dull ache deepening in my back. If I stand for a long time, it starts to throb back there like a second heartbeat. I take one more look at the tower, pray-ing it will hang on for eleven more days. Then I flip up my hood and head home.

Dad's waiting for me when I get in. "Where'd you go?" he asks.

At first I smile. It's kind of cool that he was worried about me. "Don't worry," I say. "I turned right."

He nods. "Did you go to the pond? How's that ice?" he says. "Think that tower will last awhile?" The smile falls off my face. He's worried all right—about five hundred bucks in prize money.

Lying in bed later, on my side like always, I stare at the alarm clock: angry red numbers that won't stop changing. It gets later and later. School gets closer and closer.

THE LIBRARY

I DECIDE TO VOLUNTEER in the library during lunch on Tuesday. I know it's not a long-term solution, I can't alphabetize books forever, but for now it's somewhere to go. I'm not allowed to eat in the library, so I eat a gluey tuna fish sandwich in the librarian's office before I start shelving. Then I go to the library to get to work. Ms. Verdi is out there trying to maintain order, but the fourth graders have collaborative time, and that's always close to chaos.

When the fourth graders see me heading over, with my shirt riding up and my forward lean, the volume drops. One of the boys leans over and says something to his friends. I can't quite hear it, but everyone starts laughing.

Ms. Verdi tells them to quiet down.

I stare at the boy who said something. He smiles up at me, invulnerable. He's already more popular than I'll ever be.

There's nothing left to do but get to work. I start pushing the cart around and shelving books. I'm always really interested in what books people are reading here. A lot of the books I'm putting back are ones that I've read too: *Harry Potter*, *I Survived*, *Timmy Failure*, *The Lord of the Rings*.

I think about that for a while. Most of these kids ignore me, and some do worse than that—but we still like the same books. We've imagined fighting the same epic battles and laughed at the same jokes.

Shelving takes concentration. You need to remember what books you've got and match them with the right section, the right letter. You can kind of get lost in it. But as I push the cart toward the other end of the library, I hear a loud metal clank, followed by laughter.

It's coming from the maker space. It's in a room just like Ms. Verdi's office but on the opposite end of the library. There's a window looking out, just like in hers. The blinds are down but the slats are open. There are a bunch of kids in there. At the head of the table, I see the beanpole body and enormous black-framed glasses of our science teacher, Mr. Feig.

Our maker space is kind of a volunteer effort. Mostly Mr. Feig runs it during his free period, and sometimes other teachers will pinch-hit. No one can be in there alone because of all the sharp edges and the imminent threat of, like, gluing your hands together.

I push my cart closer and lean in for a better look through the blinds. Heads are down and hands are busy. I see a wrench, a screwdriver: actual tools. I see Landrover wrestling with something large and metallic, but fortunately he doesn't see me. Nephi is sitting on the far side of the long table, bent over something that looks like a fish tank and working with a pair of wire cutters. He's super focused, like usual, but suddenly he looks up. I'm caught spying, cold busted. I lift my chin weakly, a reverse nod, and before he has a chance to react, I get back to shelving.

Toward the end of the period, the boy who made the joke walks up to me. His face is really serious, so I get serious too. He's holding an old, thick book that looks huge in his hands. He's got two friends trailing behind him. "Sorry about before," says the boy. "I didn't mean anything by it."

I size him up, trying to figure out his angle. He's just a kid, with a little boy's haircut and a shirt that says "Live Every Week Like It's Shark Week." *I like sharks too*, I think. "That's cool, man," I say. "No big deal."

I'm trying to be cool—I'm trying *really hard* to be cool enough for this fourth grader. It's pathetic, but I think I pull it off.

"Okay, thanks," he says.

I smile, and he begins to walk away. "Oh!" he says, like he forgot something. "Here's one more book to put back on the shelf. I think you missed it."

He hands me the book he's been holding. I look down at it as he walks away with his friends. It's *The Hunchback of Notre-Dame* by Victor Hugo. I'm totally blindsided. I've read it. Of course I've read it. This book is like the bane of my existence—the book and the stupid cartoons and movies it has spawned over the years. Frickin' Quasimodo.

You probably know the name, even if you've never been called it on a playground. He's the guy in the title. His job is to ring the bells of Notre-Dame Cathedral, and he's got all kinds of problems. He's honestly written more like an animal than a person. And because he's so "hideous" and "monstrous" and everyone is so mean to him, he completely loses it over a pretty girl who's nice to him for like one hot second. It's a good story and super dramatic, but the characters are all kind of stubborn and one-dimensional. I think that's the word. What I mean is they're all just one main thing. The ugly bell-ringer, the pretty girl, the vain captain of the guard . . .

Except in this book, they aren't saved by who they are. They're destroyed by it. Doomed by their looks, ruined by their vanity. No one changes at all, and no one learns anything—it's depressing!

The fleshy slap of high fives snaps me back to reality. I look up and see the three fourth graders walking away, shaking visibly as they try not to crack up. I can feel my face burning, turning red. I look down at the book, trying to comprehend what just happened. It's not a kids' book, not at all, but everyone has heard of it, so he must have gone looking for it in the Advanced Reader section. Just to give it to me.

Just to make fun of me.

I can't help but be a little impressed. Innocent on the outside, devious on the inside . . . The kid's got a brilliant career as a serial killer ahead of him.

"Did Jerome apologize?" I hear.

I hide the book behind my back as I turn around. It's Ms. Verdi.

"Huh?" I say. "Jerome?"

"I told him to come over here and apologize for what he said before."

What exactly *did* he say? I wonder.

"Did he apologize?" she repeats.

"Yeah," I say. "Sure."

"Good," she says.

I stand there for a few long seconds. I can feel the book's weight behind my back. This stupid book . . . I sort of want to show it to her, to tell her. But snitching on a fourth grader? I just can't do it. She's looking at me now, waiting. I have to say something. I just blurt out the first thing I think of: "What's going on in the maker space? I didn't know we could sign in during lunch."

"Normally, no," she says. "We've always held maker space during study hall. But with the Building a Better Norton contest going on, we wanted to give kids extra time to work on their models."

Nephi and the others are filing out of the back room now. I know at least some of them are regulars during study hall—but giving up their lunch? They must be really into this contest.

"You could sign in next time," says Ms. Verdi.

I look at her closely. Does she know I'm avoiding the cafeteria? Can she see how much I need somewhere else to be? "Maybe," I say. The truth is, I tried maker space a few times before. I've always liked building things. I still play *Minecraft* sometimes, and when I was a little kid I was the LEGO *king.* But the regulars in there are a tight-knit group. I felt like a cat in a dog run—even more than usual.

"Thanks for the help today, Ked," she says, turning to go. "You always do such a good job shelving."

"Thanks," I say as she walks away. I take the book from behind my back. "Just one more to go."

ALL OF IT, OR YOU'RE GONE

AFTER SCHOOL, I play Xbox until it starts to get dark out. I don't bother to get up and turn on the lights. I have a lot of blowing-stuff-up to get out of my system. Many suckers get light-sabered. Just as I'm about to respawn for the umpteenth time, I hear shouting out in the yard. The words are muffled by the insulated window glass, but I recognize both voices. Dad wasn't careful enough, and Mr. K caught him. This is bad.

I get up and walk over to the window, my legs stiff from sitting for so long. I look down from behind the dark window, and now I'm glad I never turned on the lights. I can see them standing there like two gray ghosts on the patchy white snow. They are both shouting at once, both waving their arms around in big violent gestures.

I reach down and quietly crack open the window. I hold my breath and listen to what they're saying. It isn't good.

"Heartless?" Mr. K shouts. "You think I don't need that money for anything? The mortgage, for one. You're delinquent!"

Dad shakes his head and sputters: "I'm just a little—"

"Yeah, you're always just a little," shouts the landlord, cutting him off. "Just a little short, just a little late—just about the worst tenant I ever had!"

It's rough hearing your dad get yelled at like this. It makes me feel mad and embarrassed and helpless all at once.

"Just give me a little more time!" Dad shouts, not like a question at all. And that's how I know for sure he doesn't have this month's rent, and since it's pretty early in the month for this kind of showdown, that means he didn't pay last month's either. My heart drops. We owe at least two months' rent.

"You've got till tomorrow!" says Mr. K. "For all of it!"

"Give me till the eighteenth!"

Why the eighteenth? It seems random. He's up to something—and with Dad, that's never good. I guess he's got a payday before then—every two weeks—but if we're really that far behind, that wouldn't be nearly enough.

Mr. K is just as confused. "The eighteenth?" he says, and now he's not yelling so much as just talking loudly. He takes out his phone, checks the calendar, I guess. "You want to pay on a Saturday?"

Dad is still panting from yelling, but now he pauses, considering the question. "That Monday, then," he says. "The twentieth."

"Okay, two months' worth, on the twentieth," says Mr. K. "Or you're gone."

No! You can't just kick someone out. There are laws. I don't exactly know them, but I know there's a whole process. It could at least buy us some time. I mentally beg my dad to keep putting up a fight. But if Dad gives his word . . . My dad is a screwup, but he's still got some pride left. If he makes a promise, shouting for the whole neighborhood to hear, he'll keep it.

"Yeah. We'll go," he says.

And just like that, it's over. Our heartless landlord heads one way, and the world's worst tenant heads the other. I slowly slide the window closed: *click.* A second later, I hear Dad's heavy footsteps stomping up the stairs, old boots on old wood.

He throws open the door and I'm playing Xbox with the sound up.

Pew! pew-pew! go the blasters.

Pish-shhwong! goes the lightsaber.

"I need the TV," goes the father.

He has no idea I heard.

SHORT

DAD SPENDS MOST of the night on the couch watching shows about fishing and people who live in Alaska. I watch with him for a while. I want to talk to him about this. I want to know how much of the money he has and if he has a plan for getting the rest. But I don't know how. He never really talks to me about money, and he gets mad when I ask too many questions.

I head to my room, but I'm still thinking about it. Maybe he is too. I don't know. He's just quiet, watching those fish. What I do know is this: He's asleep on the couch when I head to the kitchen later for a snack. It happens—especially since he watches sleepy-voiced shows about fishing and simple living. I was half expecting it. Maybe I was even hoping a little. I pause only long enough to take a deep breath. Any longer and I won't do it. I need answers, and I think I know where to find them.

I head toward Dad's room.

One more look back. His head is lolled to the side, eyes closed, his face lit by the TV. I open the door to his room, slip inside, and close it softly behind me.

It's dark and smells like a bear cave. I have no choice: I flip the light switch. If he wakes up now, he could see the light under the door. I never thought I'd do this, never thought I'd go this far. I look around the room and spot the little metal box on top of the dresser where he keeps the rent money. The fact that it's always in cash tells you something already. This is an under-the-table thing, another cut-rate deal in a town full of them.

I need to know how short we are, how bad it is. My pulse is pounding in my ears as I walk quietly across the room in my socks. The rent box is next to a junk-filled bowl that's painted like an Easter egg and used to be Mom's. It feels like a crime as soon as I touch the box. I shouldn't be doing this, but there's a momentum to it that's hard to explain. If I'm being honest, it's kind of exciting. Not fun, but electric. *I need to know.*

There's a button on the front, right under the latch. I press it, and the latch flips open. I lift the lid. Money. Not in grubby little wads like I'm expecting, but in one neatly folded stack. My hands are shaking as I start to count Dad's money. *Our money,* I correct myself. Our rent money. It looks like a big stack, like a lot. I see the hundred-dollar bill on the outside, and think: *We're fine.*

Hundred-dollar bills are so cool. But there's only one of those. Then three fifties (also cool). After that it's twenties, then tens, then a few fives. It goes fast, and when I'm done counting, we're not fine. We're short, seriously short. We don't even have enough to pay February's rent—which obviously means there's nothing for this month.

I run through the figures one more time in my head. Being poor is like always being in math class. We owe two months' rent. We have less than one. Dad has promised to pay both. His whole paycheck won't cover the difference—and that's if he hasn't already taken an advance against it, like he usually does when he's short.

What's strange is that there's usually a reason we're short. Because the car broke down or I had to go to the hospital for my back again or something like that. We are short some specific amount because of something unexpected. But not this short, and not with a running car and a back that's no worse than it was yesterday. Dad's been going to work every day, as far as I know.

I refold the money, thinking: *Where's the rest?*

And then I find out. When I go to slide the bills back inside, I see a single slip of yellow notebook paper at the bottom of the box. Oh no. I've seen one of these before. Mom found one before she left. At least one. I put the bills down next to the box, pull out the slip, and unfold it. Here's what it says:

St. Paddy's 12–4

1k 10/1

It's Dad's handwriting. Here's what that means, in case you've spent less time puzzling over my dad's notes than I have:

He bet on St. Patrick's Day, just like I did, but his bet is between noon and four o'clock. That's got to be the tower. He bet a thousand bucks and got ten-to-one odds.

That $1,000 plus his paycheck would have been more than enough for the rent. Now, if he loses, he loses it all. If he wins, we're golden, but Dad never wins. Instead, he just gambled away our home.

There's one more thing written at the bottom of the note: "SB." I know what that means too: the Stubbs brothers. That scares me. They're bookies. They take bets. It's illegal, but they have a talent for never being in jail at the same time. There's always at least one of them around to take Dad's bet—and always at least one of them to collect when he loses.

I fold the paper up and put it back in the box. I put the bills on top of it. I close it and back slowly toward the door.

I turn off the light and slip out into the living room. Dad is still asleep on the couch, his head tilted to the other side now. I close his door behind me: *click*.

He doesn't even flinch. I take a few steps away from the scene of the crime. If he looked up now, he'd never know. For a split second I think: *Now I can relax.* And honestly, that has got to be the single stupidest thought I have ever had. Relax? I am *vibrating* with shock and anger and disappointment and fear.

I want to shout at him and tell him I know and he's an idiot and maybe break the TV over his head. But this is exactly the reason Mom left us—or at least the reason she left him. So the next thought I have I can't even help: Will it be the reason he leaves too? I am so angry at him now, and so utterly aware that he's all I've got left.

So instead I just slip into my own room like I'm the thief.

10

CLASSIFIED

IT'S SNOWING WHEN I WAKE UP WEDNESDAY. **I** walk over to my window to size up any chance of a snow day, just out of habit. But I can see immediately that it's not going to happen. It's just those little flakes, not much bigger than table salt, doing a twisty dance in the wind. God is salting us.

Last night comes back to me. Looking out at the snow, I have to face some hard facts. Dad isn't just hoping to win that money. He's counting on it. That's why he asked Mr. K for the eighteenth—the day after St. Paddy's. I can practically hear him now: *I've got a good feeling about this* or *It can't miss* or any of the other dumb things he says.

I put my palm up against the windowpane. It is freezing out there. *That tower* might *make it to St. Paddy's,* I think, but then I shake the thought away. I can't fall into that. I can't be like him. When my mom left, she left me too. I don't know why, but I know what she used to say to me sometimes: "You're so much like your father."

It's time to start getting ready. The school doesn't want me either, but it has to take me. I grab my backpack and stuff my homework inside. Sometimes I walk by Dad's door and whisper "Bye," but I don't today. I just head down the stairs and out into the light, swirling snow. It's one of those March days in Maine where it feels like winter will never end.

School feels the same way: endless. It also feels kind of pointless. All day it's like there's a pane of glass between me and my classes. How can I worry about a test when I could be homeless soon? But I get through, and the final bell rings. On the way home, I stop in the pharmacy. I still have some money from last week's bottles and cans, and I want to buy some candy. I just want to feel a little better, even if it's only for the duration of a Snickers bar.

But as I walk past the counter I see that this week's local paper is out and I get a total brainstorm. The paper has classified ads in the back—maybe I could get a job! Something quick or something that pays up front.

I pool up all my change and buy the *Norton News*. I know I could read it for free at the library, but this feels like a secret. I want to be able to take my time with it and cut things out.

I don't have to check to see if the coast is clear on the way home or worry that there will be a big old padlock keeping me out. Instead, when I get there, it's like there's an invisible clock hanging over the whole place. The full rent by the twentieth or we're gone.

Inside, I get a Pop-Tart and plop down on the couch. I open the paper and flip straight to the classified ads in the back. The

"Help Wanted" section is all the way at the end, and before I even get there something else catches my eye. Two words that feel like they were meant for me: "NEED MONEY?!"

I read the rest:

"NEED MONEY?! CAN'T MISS BIZ OP!"

Biz op? It sounds like a space blaster in a sci-fi movie: *Biz-op!* But then I get it: Business Opportunity. I keep reading:

"Vintage Rd R-kit. Needs wrk bt grt valu! Fix it! Sell it! Profit!!! Srious offers only."

And that's it, except for a phone number. I read it again. It's the word "kit" that I latch onto. I don't know what an R-kit is, but I know a kit is something you put together. Dad's got some old tools around here somewhere. I like to build things—and I definitely "NEED MONEY?!" A bizarre idea starts to form in my tiny lizard brain. I know from the start that it's basically impossible. It says right there "Srious offers only," and I sriously have nothing to offer.

I flip to the help-wanted ads and scan the page. It's all adult stuff, like "account supervisor" and "bookkeeper." I can't imagine anyone hiring me for those. Even more depressing is the "Services Offered" section right after that. Just a bunch of down-on-their-luck dudes offering to paint your house or fix your sink for "lowest rates around!!!" I guess that's where I would fit in, but these guys already beat me to it—and who's going to let me anywhere near their sink?

It's a total washout. *I tried*, I think. And then, very slowly, I flip back to that first ad. I stare at it for a while before deciding to take the next step and at least get some more information. What's an R-kit, anyway?

We don't have internet at home anymore, otherwise I could've read the paper online. We had to give up that or cable, and Dad makes weird decisions. No Xbox Live for me. It's basically a medieval existence. I don't have a cell phone anymore either. (I used to have an "emergency" one but it broke.) It's embarrassing. Almost everyone else in my grade has one. I do have advanced-level knowledge of all the public computers in town, though. I tear the ad out and leave the rest of the paper there like a gutted fish. Then I pick my jacket up off the floor and head to the public library.

The Norton Public Library looks like a normal house, except for the sign out front and the wheelchair ramp. Those make it look more like a dentist's office. It's just a low, squat building with grimy white siding, but it's still my favorite place in town. Inside, they can get you pretty much any book in the state of Maine through interlibrary loan. It's like magic. Book magic. I use it a lot.

I walk up the ramp when I get there. I grab the handrail and whip myself around the turn. The library is full of people when I open the door. All four computers are full too. I'm definitely not the only one without internet at home around here.

I print my name nice and clear on the sign-up sheet so there's no confusion, and then I kill time flipping through graphic novels. I'm too wired for anything else. I'm impatient and my knee is pumping up and down in a way that I know annoys people. I can't help it.

When my turn finally arrives, I shoot over to the computers like a missile. I'm hovering over this guy's shoulder as he's collecting his stuff and I look down and see his résumé on top of the pile. For adults, a résumé is like the report card of their life. It says where they worked, where they went to school, if they graduated first in their class or got promoted at their last job—things like that. It's what people use to get jobs.

It's what my mom used to get her new job in the wrong Portland, not that she ever told us she was sending it out of state. But just one quick glance and I can tell that this guy's résumé is more like my dad's, where the "Education" section starts and stops at high school, and the "Employment" section is mostly some failing factory. My mom got "inspired" and started emailing her résumé all over the place. Sometimes my dad gets "fed up" and mails his like one town over.

Those are the words they use, anyway, but I honestly think they should reverse them. It was my mom who got fed up—with my dad, with this town, with me, maybe—and it's my dad who gets inspired sometimes. His horizons just aren't all that high, or that far.

The guy gets up and slides past me. He looks at my back and then at my face. I can see him trying to put it together—hundred-year-old back, twelve-year-old face—but he looks away quick and doesn't say anything. He's pretty old and smells like he hasn't washed in a few days. No computer, no shower, no job . . . I wonder if he's homeless. And then I wonder if I'll have more in common with him soon than just sharing this computer. The thought gives me a sick, wobbly feeling, like the moment in between losing control of your bike and hitting the ground.

I slide into the chair and take his place.

When your computer access comes a half hour at a time, you get pretty good at finding things quickly. What I find, almost immediately, is that a Rd R-kit isn't a kit at all.

I type it in and right away the search engine wants to know: "*Did you mean* Road Rokkit?"

Did I?

I click on that and I really hope it's right, because this thing is SWEET. It's one of those minibikes and, like, mini-er than most. Some of the entries call them "pocket bikes" because they're so small. I am looking at pictures of dudes hunched over on Road Rokkits, their knees up to their chests and the bike barely visible between their legs. They look like monkeys riding tricycles in a circus, elbows out trying to balance over this tiny machine, but then I find some videos and they really are rocketing down the road.

The other thing I notice is that a lot of the videos are old, like noticeably low-def. It's not hard to figure out why. Every page seems to say "Rare" or "Vintage" right at the top, almost like it's part of the thing's name: Rare Road Rokkit, Vintage Road Rokkit . . . There's even a Road Rokkit Museum in California. I click on that and find out why. They stopped making these things almost a decade ago. The youngest Road Rokkit is almost as old as me!

But they're still super popular. The museum page says they've got "a cult following." So why did they stop making them?

After watching a video called "Epic Road Rokkit Wrekks" with these guys perched like parrots atop these tiny bikes going from zero to thirty in about three seconds and then going from thirty to zero in an instant, the answer is clear. They are ridiculously dangerous.

I type in my next search, "Road Rokkit for Sale," and I just about fall out of my seat. People are paying four, five, six hundred bucks for these things! There's even a mint-condition one from 1998 going for a thousand dollars!

I only have a few minutes of computer time left. I reach into my pocket and count how much change I have left. I find some good, info-dense pages and hit print. It's ten cents a page here, so I only print five pages. I'll look for cans again tonight.

The next guy is already waiting as my time runs out, so I get up, get my printouts, and pay at the front desk. It's the younger librarian and she is friendly as usual and wearing a flowery dress like it's already spring. "Doing some homework?" she says.

"Research," I say. And then, I don't know why, maybe because she's pretty and has big green eyes, I add: "Business opportunity." I pause dramatically, like I'm James Bond: "Can't miss."

She nods very seriously and says, "Don't forget us when you're rich."

I want to say something smooth, like, *How could I ever forget you?* Instead, I grin like an idiot and sort of gurgle out a laugh. So smooth.

The wind hits me in the face and nearly tears the papers right

out of my hand when I push my way out the library doors. I fold
the papers into a lump and put them in the big inside pocket of
my parka. But when I turn up the street, the wind is suddenly
with me and it pushes me toward home. It feels like a sign. There
is literally an invisible force pushing me forward. If I did something risky now, something big—it's almost like it wouldn't even
be my fault. Almost like it might even work.

11

MAKING THE CALL

DAD STILL ISN'T HOME when I get back. Even though I'm inside now and I've left the wind behind, it still feels like I'm being pushed forward somehow. I dial the number from the ad before I can chicken out. We still have a landline because it comes free with the cable. I pace a little, waiting for someone to answer.

Just as I decide that this is nuts and start to pull the phone away from my ear to hang up, I hear a voice. "Yeah?"

I just look at the phone in my hand.

"Hello?" I hear, a tiny, tinny voice floating through the air.

I raise the phone back to my ear. "Yes," I hear myself say. That first word sort of squeaks out, but after that I try to make my voice sound deeper, more adult. "I'm calling about the business opportunity?"

There's a pause. I feel light-headed.

"The—? You mean the bike?"

"It's a Road Rokkit, right?"

"Yeah."

"How much?" I blurt.

"Well, it's kind of old. They don't even make 'em anymore, you know?"

"I know," I whisper.

"But a friend of mine told me that some people are still into 'em."

People are *really* into them, but I don't say anything because I don't want to give anything away. The man keeps talking. "I don't know why. These things are really dangerous. It was okay when the kids were younger. They're indestructible at that age, you know? But now?"

"How much?" I say again.

"It needs work."

"I know."

The man pauses. Part of me is afraid he's reconsidering, and part of me is afraid he isn't.

"I'll tell you what," he says at last. "Two hundred bucks and it's yours."

My head is still reeling, but having something to concentrate on helps. I do the math. It sounds like this thing is definitely not mint condition, so a thousand bucks is out. But if I fix it up nice, maybe six hundred? And it's so small, how long could it take? I fixed my own bike once. Well, I helped Dad, but I'm the one who got the chain back on. So six minus two . . . I'd make four hundred bucks. Add in one more paycheck from Dad . . .

It would be enough to cover the rent we owe.

"You there?" he says. "You hear me?"

"Yes," I say. "It's a deal. What's your address? How soon can I pick it up?"

He gives me the address. It's close.

I leave the hundred-dollar bill on the outside of the stack. I even leave the first fifty, but I take the other two. The rest I take in twenties. Then I fold the bills over again, super careful, and put them back just the way I found them. The stack is definitely thinner now, but dad would have to pick it up to notice. He might even have to recount it.

I know it's a risk. The thing is, sometimes, when you've got a business opportunity, you need a loan. *A short-term loan*, I tell myself. And hopefully it won't attract too much interest.

12

THE EDGE OF TOWN

I AM IN MY ROOM with the door closed because I don't trust myself not to act guilty. Dad is in the living room. I couldn't put the money back now even if I wanted to.

Instead, I go to my desk and find an envelope. My mom gave me a whole box of them so that I could write her letters. I still have most of my box of envelopes, and she definitely still has most of hers. I slip the money inside. With the two fifties on top, it looks like a bribe in a movie.

I go to the living room and try to sound casual as I ask Dad if I can go for another walk. He is half-asleep on the couch. I think maybe I woke him up when I came out of my room.

If he says no, that will be the end of it. I'll go back to my room and sneak the money back into the rent box tomorrow. There are so many things wrong with this plan, things I'm just starting to think of now that I've had some more time. It would almost be a relief to give it up.

"Turn right," he says.

It feels like fate, but it's not. It's a decision he made, a decision I'm making.

I walk out the door and when I reach the sidewalk, for the first time, I turn left.

I start walking, and here's the thing: I don't have to walk far. Things start to change fast. I guess I didn't realize how close we lived to the edge of town. Maybe I was trying not to think about it? Maybe I'm an idiot? I've learned from experience that both of those can be true at the same time.

Sure, I knew we hit the edge of town right away in the car— but that's a car. I'm walking now, and still: The houses get more broken-down with every block, and the yards get more cluttered. I don't know if the edge of town has an official starting point, but I see a doorless refrigerator lying in the middle of a lawn with a stolen shopping cart sticking out, and that seems like a good candidate.

I look back over my good side and I can still see the lights from my neighborhood, just a normal neighborhood where kids go trick-or-treating and you don't feel like you have to look both ways to walk down the sidewalk.

Mr. K said he'd kick us out if we didn't pay what we owe, and now I'm starting to understand where we'd go. How close we already are.

The urge to retreat is strong. I pass a big, square house with boarded-up windows. It's as dark as a black hole inside: No light escapes. There probably hasn't been electricity in there for years.

I wonder if people still live there, in the dark like moles living underground. Or with candles maybe, just daring the dirty old place to burn down. There are always fires in the news, and places like this are why.

I hear something move, a quick thump along the side of the house. I freeze defensively, possum up, and stare in that direction. I don't see anything. *Must've been the wind,* I tell myself as I start walking again. But as I reach the end of the yard I hear it again: *Thump!*

I shift gears and turbo-boost down the block. The idea of getting attacked out here is scary. The thought of someone taking this money is terrifying. The next house is low and flat with a wire fence. There's a battered snowmobile in the yard with no handlebars. An old car is parked along the street out front, alongside a rusty chain-link fence. The house has dirty white siding with dark smears running down, like it was wearing makeup and has been crying. No lights on here either, but at least this one has windows. I look into the dark black squares and wonder if anyone is looking out.

I walk along the curb and feel a crunch beneath my boots. I look down and see little bits of broken glass on the ground, glowing in the light from the moon and the nearest working streetlight. Someone broke into a car here.

I look at the house's black windows again and see something shift in the darkness inside—a curtain? A person? I speed up. I make it two blocks, huffing and puffing the whole way, but then

I see what I'm looking for: a sign that says Hornbeam Road. I take the folded paper from my coat pocket and check the address: *59 Hornbeam Road.*

I follow the numbers from the corner. It's a big old pile of a place three houses down. There's only one streetlight working on this block, but it's the one right in front of where I'm going. I stand underneath it, sizing the place up. I can't decide if the light makes me safer or just an easier target.

The house has a few too many doors and windows for its size, and the roof is slanting too much to one side, like a barn out in the country. The whole place looks out of whack, like something out of *Alice in Wonderland.* But there are lights on and smoke is coming from the chimney. I take a deep breath and head up the walkway.

The welcome mat says "Get Lost," but I feel like I already am. I can't believe I came here with two hundred dollars! As I press the doorbell, I'm imagining myself tied up in the basement with duct tape over my mouth. There's a harsh, electric buzz.

The door flies open almost instantly. There's a big dude standing there. He must have been waiting. His beard and sweater are both brown and so ragged that it's hard to tell where one stops and the other begins. *Next stop, basement.*

"You here about the bike?" he says.

"Yeah," I squeak.

He looks at me closer, narrowing his eyes. With my parka on, he can't see my back clearly, but he can tell something's going on under there. Then I see the light come on in his eyes. "I know you," he says. "I mean, I've seen you around."

"Yep," I say. "That's me."

Having any kind of visible, you know, thing going on in a small town is like a weird sort of celebrity. The man raises his head and looks out into the night behind me. "Well, I'm Wade," he says. "Your, uh, parents out in the car or something?"

It doesn't seem like a good idea to tell this mountain man–looking dude that I'm alone. "My dad's circling the block," I say. "I've got the money."

"Right down to business, huh?" he says. His tone is friendlier than before, like he's joking with me. But I'm serious.

"Yep," I say.

"Well, I've got the bike." He looks behind him, back into the hallway. I can see a small table near the door, some picture frames on the walls. It doesn't look as much like a Murder House as I expected—and do murderers tell you their name? I guess they might—if they're going to murder you anyway. "You want to come in?"

"No!" I say, maybe a little too fast. "I'll just wait here."

"Suit yourself," says Wade. He closes the door most of the way and disappears back into the house. I look around the front of the house as I wait. I see a flicker of light from a second-floor window just above me, but by the time I turn to look all I see is a yellow curtain fluttering closed. Was someone watching me? The door swings open again, and I jump. The guy doesn't notice because he's doubled over holding on to the handlebars of this tiny little minibike.

I look down at it, horrified. The frame is beat up. The red paint is chipped in some places and gone in others. Worst of all, there's a big hole in the middle.

"Uh, where's the engine?" I say. This is a lot more work than I expected. I was picturing something more like my old bike, with a slipped chain and bent handlebars.

"Right!" he says, pushing the bike halfway out the door and disappearing back inside.

I take hold of the handlebars as he lets go. He returns with an old bag and holds it up for me to see. It looks like the sort of dark cloth sack that you'd find a severed head in. "I was going to reconnect it, but . . ."

I stare at it, dumbfounded. I mean, I knew the bike wasn't mint condition, but the engine is literally in a dirty old sack. "I don't know," I say.

"Use your imagination," says Wade, the mountain man. "Look at this frame."

I look down at the frame.

"What don't you see?"

"An engine?" I venture.

"Ha! Good one," he says. "The correct answer is rust."

I look again. It's true. There's not much paint left, but there's no rust either. I guess that's important. "And the engine works?" I say, looking skeptically at the sack.

"Not right now," he says, "but I don't think it's anything major. I was going to fix it myself. But who has time? Two kids in high school and one in eighth."

Eighth grade—I wonder if I know him. I glance back up at the window.

"Had some vinyl," he adds. "Fixed the seat. Nice, right?"

I look back down at the seat. The seat looks almost new, and the little fat-donut tires still have some tread too. I do like he says and try to imagine this thing racing down the road. I try to imagine this thing selling for six hundred bucks.

I unzip my parka enough to reach into the inside pocket. I pull out the envelope. What can I say? I have a powerful imagination.

Wade opens the envelope and counts it. I look away, guilty. "All there," he says. He peers into the night behind me again. "You sure you're okay getting home?" he says.

"My dad is just around the corner," I lie.

He nods and hands me the bag. It's heavy but manageable. From what I saw online, these things aren't much different than a lawn mower engine. "Good luck," he says, swinging the door shut. "Wear a helmet."

I pull open the bag and look inside. Looks like machinery, anyway. I close it up and put it in my backpack. My back is already starting to ache, and the extra weight definitely doesn't help.

"Just get home," I tell myself. "Just get home." It's almost like a prayer.

And then I bend over and begin to wheel my brand-new broken minibike back toward the pre-apocalyptic part of town. My back aches and I'm sweating and breathing hard the whole way. Bent over and with my hood down, I can barely see where I'm going or who might be waiting. The wheels roll smoothly, but with no engine to connect to, the loose drive-chain rattles and clinks. The noise gives me away, and I'm sure something bad is going to happen.

But the next thing I know, I pass the junked refrigerator, and I'm back in my neighborhood. *My neighborhood for now.* It seems incredible that the key to staying here might be the hunk of "vintage" junk rolling along beside me, but I have to believe that.

I look up to make sure Dad's not looking out the window, then wheel the bike around the house and into the lawn mower shed. There's a tarp over the hibernating mower, and I tuck the frame in under it. The engine is still in my pack, and I take that inside to see what I'm dealing with.

I'm hoping Dad will be asleep on the couch when I push through the door, the heavy pack digging into my throbbing back. But he's awake and waiting for me. My knees nearly buckle. *He knows I took the money!* I can't decide if I should make a break for my room or run back down the stairs.

"How's that tower looking?" he says.

Oh. That.

"Cold night," I say, which is true.

He nods, satisfied. I guess he needs to believe in his own dumb plan too. I head straight for my room, open my door, and pause. "Hey, Dad," I say, trying to sound casual. "Where are your old tools? Got a project for school."

"Sold 'em," he says.

Blacking out in 3-2-1 . . .

But then I remember—I just saw a bunch of tools the other day: in maker space. I wasn't planning to head back there. I'm not in the contest, and it violates one of my main rules for survival: Avoid bears, live wires, and Landrover Jones.

GARBAGE TRUCK

WHEN LUNCH COMES AROUND, my whole grade heads to their lockers before heading up the hill. It's cold again, and people are wearing their jackets. I guess that's good—a better chance the tower will last the week. But I can't think like that, can't be like Dad and rely on dumb luck. I grab my parka and my old backpack.

"What the heck?" I say as I lift it up. There's a dark, greasy stain that has turned the faded blue bag black at the bottom. I brought the engine to school, and it must be leaking.

"What's that, a diaper bag?"

I don't even know who says it, because all of seventh is shuffling by me.

A few people laugh. I feel my face get hot. It does kind of look like that.

I rustle around in the mess at the bottom of my locker and find an old plastic shopping bag. I drop the pack inside, and even through the white plastic you can see the slick black stain.

Once we reach the upper building, I keep my eyes on Mr. Feig near the front of the line. Sure enough, as soon as we're all inside, he raises his hand and says, "Where my makers?"

I raise my free hand but drop it quick when no one else does. Instead, I just shuffle over and join the little group forming alongside the line. I keep my head low and look around from under my hair. I feel like I should be running the other way. Haley's there, her nose still a little bruised along the bridge. Landrover is talking to his friends Gino and Dunk and hasn't spotted me yet. I wonder if he'll be surprised or angry or even care at all when he does.

At least Nephi is here. Maybe I could say something to him? If he talks to me, it might even help me with the others. He's a regular. Just *Hey, Neff* or something simple like that. It has to be casual enough that if he doesn't answer, it's not a big deal. We haven't really talked in a while.

But before I can say anything to him, Landrover looks up. "What're you doing here, Freak?" His voice is a deep, low rumble. He keeps it just above a whisper so none of the teachers hear over the noise of the line.

I push my shoulders up and back out of some weird defensive reflex, but I still don't look him in the eyes. I guess it makes sense that he'd be here. His dad owns the auto parts store, which is like adult maker space if you think about it. It's a good job in a town like this, where everyone has old cars that are always breaking down. Landrover always has the newest, coolest stuff.

"I just, um—" I mumble.

"Nice bag," he says, cutting me off. "That your lunch?"

"It's his diaper bag!" says Gino.

I turn my head slightly to see if Nephi is witnessing this, but he's huddled with a few of the other regulars.

"Hey, I'm talking to you," says Landrover, but this time he says it loud enough for Mr. Feig to hear. He's one of my favorite teachers. Last week in science class, he filled a balloon with hydrogen and ignited it. Poof: instant fireball. So he's used to handling explosive situations.

"And I'm talking to you!" he calls cheerily. "Let's move out!"

There are a bunch of us now, and we all turn and follow Mr. Feig to the library. I hustle up and put a few bodies between me and Landrover.

When we reach the maker space door, there's already a group of eighth graders waiting. Mr. Feig opens the door, and they cut in front of us. One of them is a tall girl whose hair is black with bright purple streaks. Her clothes are black, and her nails are too. I don't know her name, but I know the word people call her. She's a goth—pretty much the only one in our school. It's only when she shoots me a nasty look that I realize I'm staring. Her hair is just really interesting, you know?

Most of the room is taken up by a long table. Some of the kids I know, some I don't. We sign in and the seats fill fast, like the music just stopped. My heart starts to pound. I don't want to sit near Landrover or Haley. I look around for Nephi, but he's sitting with the same two dudes he was talking with before. The goth girl already has the spot I wanted in the back corner.

There are still three open seats in the center of the side near the door. I head that way. I don't know the people sitting on either side that well. A girl named Chrissie is on the left and one of the four Joes in my grade is on the right. It feels a little weird to pick one to sit next to. Instead, I take the middle seat. I put my plastic bag down with a thunk, take off my parka, and put it over the back of the chair. I smooth out both my shirts and make sure nothing's riding up. Finally, I sit down and take a look around.

There are two empty seats at the table, and they are the ones on either side of me. I am radioactive. This is starting to feel a lot like the caf.

Everyone pulls out their lunches, so I get the paper bag out of my Royston's bag. "Mmmm, diapers," says Landrover. Gino laughs. I pretend I don't hear.

I eat my sandwich (bologna and cheese) and little bag of chips slowly so that I can watch the others and see what to do.

"You brought in the form last time, right?" Mr. Feig says to me right as I take a bite.

"Mmm-hmm," I say through a mouthful of sandwich. He's got a good memory. It was some kind of legal form to let the school off the hook in case I mangle myself in here. Dad signed it without even reading it.

"Excellent!" he says. "Lose as many fingers as you want."

I hear a few kids laugh and try to join in, spraying some crumbs. *Ha-ha! Lost fingers!*

The table is covered with a heavy plastic sheet, and as I run my fingers over it I can feel little splotches of dried glue and thin cuts from sharp blades. I look around the room slowly, hiding my eyes under my hair and trying to be subtle about it. I'm surprised by how many different kinds of kids are in here. One by one, they start setting their lunches aside and getting to work.

They head over to a tall metal cabinet against the back wall that Mr. Feig has just unlocked and take their models out. The contest is next weekend, so a lot of the projects are already taking shape. I see models made of tubes, boards, wires, papier-mâché. Landrover slides a huge slab of metal out of the cabinet and grabs a monkey wrench.

It's time for me to get started. I have to get the engine running if I'm going to be able to sell the bike. I want to get to the library, watch some YouTube engine repair clips, and things like that, but in the meantime, I can at least get it cleaned up and sort of, you know, assess the situation.

I throw my lunch bag out in the garbage can in the corner. On the way back, I see a roll of rough brown paper next to some tape and glue in the center of the table. I grab the roll and tear off a long sheet, rolling it around my hand until I have enough. When I get back to my seat, I tear the brown paper into strips and make a kind of place mat in front of my spot.

I feel eyes on me as I reach inside the greasy plastic bag and open the top of the cloth sack. I feel like a mad scientist about to lift a brain from a jar. The metal engine is cold, greasy-slick, and a little heavy as I lift it out. It's smaller than a lawn mower engine but more complex. I've got to say, it's pretty cool.

"Uh, Ked? What is that?" says Mr. Feig.

"It's a broken motor," I say.

"You know this isn't a garage, right?"

Suddenly, I'm afraid he won't let me work on it in here. I begin rattling off my excuses rapid-fire. "It's small! There's plastic on the table! I made a place mat!"

"It's a fire hazard," he says. My heart sinks. "And you absolutely may not start it up in here." But when I look over at him, I see that he's smiling. "You may, however, work on it, using the proper safety precautions."

I can't help it—I grin. I gently lower the little engine onto the table, and the brown paper blackens around it.

The room is completely quiet for a few moments. I know everyone is looking at the engine, and I honestly feel kind of proud of what I'm hoping to do. I think it's cool.

"Beep! Beep! Beep!" It's Landrover, and for a second I have no idea where he's going with this.

But Gino does. I guess he's more clever than I thought. "Beep! Beep! Beep!" he repeats. "Here comes the garbage truck!"

The room explodes in laughter.

"Back it up to the dump!" calls Haley, and even though it's *the exact same joke* people still laugh.

"That's enough!" calls Mr. Feig.

The laughter gets quieter but doesn't quite stop.

I look over at Nephi. He's not laughing, but his friends are. He's just giving me a look. It's not angry, exactly, but I can read his thoughts so clearly. *Don't do this to me. Don't follow me in here and ruin this for me.*

And he's right too, because I know him. He's going to feel like he has to stick up for me and tell his friends to shut it. I'm going to cost him something in here, in this place that he found for himself. When I first met Nephi, when his family first came here, he stuck out—and that's not necessarily a good thing here. He wore crisply ironed khakis and bright polo shirts and even tucked them in. He looked so serious, so—I don't even know what the word is—*formal*, maybe? He kind of spoke the same way. *For me it is that way too*, he'd say, instead of just *Me too*. But he dresses like everyone else now. And when he finally says something, he'll sound like everyone else too. But his mind is still really neat, really tucked in, if that makes any sense. Nephi likes everything to fit. This place is perfect for him, and he's perfect for it. I don't want to make him stand out again. And so I do the only thing I can.

Just as he's turning toward his friends, just as he's about to open my mouth, I open my mouth first.

I open my mouth, and I laugh at myself.

"Ha-ha-ha!" I laugh. "Garbage truck! Special delivery!"

The whole room erupts in a fresh round of laughter. From the back corner, the goth girl joins in, louder than the others: "Beep! Beep! Beep!" Mr. Feig throws up his hands in frustration. I just sit there trying hard to look like I don't care.

INTERNAL COMBUSTION

I STILL HEAR SOME WHISPERS AND SNICKERS, and I just tell myself, *So what?* They already straight-up laughed in my face. *I* laughed in my face. If they are still talking about me, who cares? It's like flicking me in the ear after punching me in the head.

My goal is to look for damage to the engine and figure out why it's not running. The first step is finding the leak. It doesn't take long. A cap on the fuel tank is missing. That's a relief. I was afraid it would be a huge hole or something. But where's the cap? I look back at the grungy bag.

I don't want to, but I reach in with my right hand and start fishing around. I feel something hard sliding around down there, and I pinch it tight and slowly pull it out. It's an oily cap.

"Dude, it's like you just pulled a bullet out of a chest cavity," says Joe, looking over. He's been sketching a complicated design on a big sheet of graph paper all class. Metal ruler, mechanical pencil: very official.

I smile, glad someone's finally talking to me. A fat drop of oil drips off my fingers and back into the bags. "It's like I'm operating," I say.

"Looks like a turd," says Gino, and I can't argue.

I rub off the oil with a paper towel and screw the cap back on. With that done, I grab another handful of paper towels and start wiping off the engine.

Once it's semi-clean, I hold it up in the light and examine it from all angles. I'm looking for cracks or any other obvious damage, but all I find is a few small dents and dings. I lean back a little and exhale. No obvious external damage. That's good.

I look around the table. No one is looking at me anymore. Everyone is busy doing their own thing. Maker space was a lot more collaborative when I was in here before, like: "Let's all work together to connect these little circuit thingies so they do something fun!" We talked about the best way to do it, and Mr. Feig sort of guided us along. I can tell right away that it's different now. It's all about the contest, and he isn't supposed to help with that. No one is. The do-it-yourself vibe is strong.

Haley is across the table, bending squares of pastel construction paper into little boxes. *Buildings*, I realize. *Houses.* The girl in black is building houses too. Hers are made of thin plastic. Guess what color? Landrover is loudly tightening something with the monkey wrench. He's got a hunk of machinery in front of him that's even larger than mine. And Nephi is working on a small, electric motor, testing things out with his fingers and carefully turning the gears before he flips the switch.

So I'm not the only one working on machinery, or even the only one with a motor. For the first time in recorded history, Landrover has made me feel like I fit in *more*.

All of their models look really good, though . . . It's intimidating. But I guess the models have to be good. There are town-wide bragging rights on the line. Whoever wins the Building a Better Norton contest will be on the morning announcements, in the paper, maybe even on the news. All I'm trying to do is rebuild a pocket bike—but I've got a lot more riding on it than the morning announcements.

I look down at the disembodied engine again, trying to visualize how it connects to the rest of the bike. The next thing I want to do is look for anything that might be too worn down: blunt gear teeth, weak connections. Mr. Feig sits down next to me just as I get started, peering down through those massive glasses of his. I'm afraid he's going to yell at me, but he stays quiet, examining the engine. Finally he says, "So, Ked. What is this? Go-kart engine?"

"Pocket bike," I say.

"You got the body of the bike squirreled away somewhere?"

I nod.

"You know what you're going to do to fix it?"

I wish I could just say yes. Instead, I tell him what I've got so far. "I think I need to find some diagrams online, plans or whatever. And I know they have these, like, fix-it videos on YouTube. But it's pretty old and they don't make this kind of bike anymore."

"The good news is that these little two-stroke engines are all pretty similar," he says.

I nod. I was kind of counting on that already. This whole time, I've had the phrase "Like a lawn mower engine" stuck in my head. I'm not sure why I find it comforting. I've never fixed one of those either. I guess it just seems like more of an everyday thing, like there'd be a lot of stuff out there on it. "I'm going to have to take it apart, huh?" I say.

"Yeah, take it apart, find the problem, put it back together." I kind of deflate in my chair. Hearing it out loud makes me realize how much work this is going to be.

"Can I use the tools in the cabinet?" I say.

"That's what they're there for," he says before getting up and walking away.

I eye the engine's metal case, trying to figure out how it comes off. I run my fingers over the screws and bolts on the front. Which ones need to come off and which ones need to stay on? Then—*WHOOMP!* Something heavy slaps down on the table next to me. Mr. Feig has dropped a thick old book: *Your Internal Combustion Engine and You.*

"Old school," says Mr. Feig. "Read up before you get started."

I should've known there'd be schoolwork. I flip the book open and turn to the section on two-stroke engines. I skim past the hedge trimmers and find the section I need: "Fixing your mini-bike: Vroom for improvement." I spend the rest of the period looking at diagrams and hoping the advice in this book is better than the jokes.

Toward the end of the period, the girl with the black and purple hair raises her hand to ask a question.

"Yes, Esme?" says Mr. Feig.

It's a nice name, but she's been pretty nasty to me, so it makes me think of a hissing snake: ESS-may. She says her X-Acto knife blade is getting dull and asks if there are more.

The warning bell rings.

"Can I borrow this?" I say, holding up the book to Mr. Feig.

"Sure," he says. "Just bring it back when you're done."

I don't look over at Landrover. I know he's there, and I know he doesn't like me, but avoiding him is just not an option right now.

I put my engine away and afterward we all file out of the library to head back down the hill. For a moment, I feel something, and I'm not even sure what it is, but it's something good.

That lasts like two minutes, of course. We're in the big hallway lining up with the lunchers filing down from the caf. I'm trying to find an open spot and maneuver my way in when I hear "Beep! Beep! Beep!"

I whip my head around. It's a girl's voice, and at first I think it's Esme again, but she's back with the eighth graders. It's Haley. Of course. I look her right in the eyes, but she doesn't stop. Her BFF Becca is with her again, and now she starts up: "Beep! Beep! Beep!"

I sure am sick of this joke, but most of the teachers have no idea what it means and just let it slide. Most of the class doesn't know what it means either. But some of them do. Up and down the line I hear chuckles, just little laughs here and there. It's the kids from maker space. They know what it means—and who it's meant for. And of course Landrover is laughing the loudest.

I want to disappear into the floor. And that's when I realize what I was feeling before, leaving the library. I felt like I was part of a group. For just a moment, I felt like I belonged somewhere. Now it feels like the opposite. My face starts to burn with embarrassment.

I shoot a look back at Haley, but she can't see me. She's turned around, explaining the joke to the girls behind her. Pretty soon the whole line will know. What's her problem? I didn't mean to hit her nose.

But it doesn't matter. Not really. I can be lonely. I can be embarrassed. I don't like it, but I've had lots of practice. What I can't be is homeless, or in some boarded-up dump on the edge of town or sharing a motel room with Dad out by the highway. That's what matters most right now. I need to fix this bike—even if I get wrecked in the process.

ENEMY TERRITORY

I'M RUNNING A LITTLE LATE on my way to maker space on Friday. I know I have to go, but it feels like enemy territory. I don't enjoy being laughed at. I don't like being around Landrover. Even if you really need the honey, you're not going to be too excited to stick your hand in the beehive.

So maybe I'm dragging my feet a little, but I'm still surprised when I pick up the clipboard and see that there's only one spot left. There were two empty seats last time, but I guess that's not much: one friend, one absence, whatever. I sign my name in the last slot. Mr. Feig walks over and takes the clipboard from my hand.

"Sorry, Landrover," he says.

Landrover? Where? I turn and look and there he is, filling the doorway behind me. Uh-oh.

"You know the deal," Mr. Feig is saying to him, "only as many spots as there are seats. Come back next time." Landrover doesn't even look at him. He's fixing me with a death stare. I'm caught in it, like a tractor beam, staring right at him as he mouths two small words: "You're dead."

Then he slides sideways out the door and disappears. The death stare flickers out, and I am released. I look around the table. There's only one seat left, and it's between Landrover's two BFFs (Bully Friends For-evil). Gino and Dunk must have been saving him a seat.

One look at them tells me they're not happy with the change of plans. Believe me, I'm not either.

I want to leave, to go back into the library and just sit there and read something. But I don't. I can't. I head over to the open metal cabinet for my engine. It's still lying there on the old towel I left it on. *Keep calm*, I tell myself as I carefully walk it over to the table. I tell myself that Landrover's friends aren't going to do anything to me with Mr. Feig right there.

But even with those space telescope glasses of his, Mr. Feig can't see under the table. As soon as I sit down, Gino delivers a sharp punch to my thigh, grinding his knuckles in at the end.

"Ow," I hiss.

Mr. Feig looks up.

Gino looks over at me, fake surprise plastered onto his face. "What happened?" he says, and now both he and Mr. Feig are waiting for my answer. He's daring me to say something. I play it out in my head.

If I say, *He hit me*, Gino will deny it. There are no witnesses, so Feig will issue a warning. I'll get the worst of both worlds: I'll snitch but won't get justice. It's really the first part that's the bigger issue. Telling on someone is considered super uncool at this school—maybe at every school. In fact, as uncool as I already am, snitching might be the only way I could sink any lower.

"Nothing," I mumble. "Cramp or something."

Gino nods, and for a brief, pathetic moment, I'm glad he approves. As soon as Mr. Feig looks away, Gino leans in.

"That's for taking Rover's spot," he snarls. It's definitely menacing, but I can't help it: I laugh. The little chuckle slips through my lips before I can press them closed.

"Something funny?" he says.

I just can't help it: "You call him *Rover*?" It just seems really funny to me. He's already named after a truck, and now his nickname sounds like a dog? That's ruff. Landrover is a total golden boy, but when it comes to names he just *cannot* catch a break. One last tiny giggle slips out, and I immediately wish it hadn't.

Gino narrows his eyes. "You are so dead."

"I know," I say, looking down at the table and doing everything I can to keep a straight face. "Rover told me."

A second later, Dunk (real name: Duncan) drills me in the other thigh. All I can do is bite my lip and take it. The punches stop after that. I don't know if they don't want to push their luck, or if they're waiting until they can hit me for real, above the table. All I know is that they're not done with me—and neither is Rover.

I try to tune it all out. I've got work to do.

The engine is in front of me on the table. I reach into my backpack and pull out a few pages I printed at the library yesterday. It's a diagram of a Road Rokkit engine. Next, I carefully pull out a ziplock bag. It's like I brought an engine-repair picnic. I peel a damp, soapy washcloth out from inside the baggie and spend a few minutes wiping any grease I missed with the paper towels off the engine. When I'm done, the washcloth is black and the engine is gleaming.

I walk back to the cabinet and get the tools I'll need. There's a regular tool kit in here, like you might have in your garage. I've gone over the diagrams, so I know what I need: the socket wrench, the Allen wrench, and a screwdriver. I grab a can of WD-40 too.

Once I have the tools, it's time to start taking the engine apart. I've already read the minibike section of the book twice, and I've got the printouts right in front of me, but this part still makes me nervous. It's just a two-stroke engine, like on a hedge trimmer or chain saw, but it's still got some small, breakable parts. I take a deep breath and get to it.

I stand up for this part. I spread my hands and wiggle my fingers to loosen them up before I start. Now I really do feel like a surgeon about to operate. The first thing I do is separate the fuel tank and carburetor from the rest of the engine. Just some unscrewing and tugging and it comes apart.

I've cracked the coconut.

I eye the carburetor nervously. That's the part that mixes the fuel with air so it will ignite. It's small and self-contained, like a heart. I know from the diagrams that there are thin rubber gaskets and other tricky little parts. Some of those pieces are delicate and I don't have replacements. There's absolutely no way I'm starting with that. I need to get used to working with the engine first and build up to it.

The rest of the engine looks more durable, like you could drop it and it would probably be fine. According to the book, the engine has a few different systems. First there's the ignition system. The spark plug sticking out of the top is scuffed up and looks pretty old. It could be dead or close to it. I mentally add a new one to my shopping list.

Then there's the compression system: the piston and the cylinder. It's the pumping heart of the bike, and that's what I start with. I find the socket size I need, put it on the socket wrench, and get cranking.

Taking it apart goes faster than I expected. There's some gunk for sure, but the little engine is not that complicated: If you see a bolt, take it off. Set it aside. Repeat. So I take off the armature coil without too much trouble. Taking off the flywheel is harder. I have to use a screwdriver as a pry bar because the thing is on a taper.

This is probably more detail than you need, but I'll be honest: I kind of want credit for it. No offense to those epic LEGO space stations, but this is by far the most complicated thing I've tried to build or rebuild.

I fit the Allen wrench through the cooling vents to take off the cylinder. It's a little tricky getting at the bolts that hold the crankcase on. And the whole time, some of the pieces are sticking a little. They're putting up a fight, but not as much as I expected. I guess all that grease and oil was good for something.

Plus, the WD-40 is amazing. It's like Super Grease, and it has a long, thin plastic barrel so you can aim it like a laser. If a bolt is really sticking or I see a scab of old gunk at the base, I give it a quick blast: *PSSST!* The smell is slick and sweet. It's not as strong as I expected, but there is definitely a whiff of every garage/workshop I've ever been in.

I look up and see Esme glaring over at me from the corner. She's giving me the total stink-eye, and I can't tell if it's the smell that bothers her or if it's just me.

Every time Mr. Feig checks in on his trips around the room, I'm afraid he's going to shout: *Stop! You're ruining it!* But mostly he just nods and says little things, like *Looking good* or *Those two pieces go together.* It feels good, like I'm doing an okay job, and it gives me the confidence to keep going.

By the time I separate the crankshaft I'm officially in that same zone I get into with LEGOs or *Minecraft.* It can be almost hypnotic, you know? Building, taking apart . . . It's like some deep part of you takes over and your eyes and hands work together perfectly and all of your loud thoughts get quiet.

And other things get quiet too. I know that Gino and Dunk are saying things to me whenever I lean down close or the room gets loud. Insults, threats—the usual, I guess. But I'm not listening. I'm in my own world, and in my world there are NO JERKS ALLOWED.

And then it's done: The engine is taken apart. For a second, I just stand there looking down at it. All the parts are laid out neatly. Now that I've drifted back to reality, I realize that my back is throbbing from standing so long bent over like that.

There's not much time left in the class, but I want to get started cleaning things up. I see a bunch of gunk on the exhaust port and check the book: It's probably carbon. I want to blast it with the WD-40, but the book says to scrape it off with the edge of a flat-head screwdriver. I figure the book knows more than I do, so I do that. I put a paper towel down and tilt the port down so the black, charcoal-looking flakes spill out of the engine and onto that.

Now that it's cracked open, I can see plenty of gunk that I couldn't get to before. Honestly, if the spark plug or the connections aren't the problem, all this crud in here could be. But there's not enough time left even for a once-over with the soapy washcloth—which is now more of an oily rag anyway.

All I can manage is putting some of the bolts and stuff in plastic sandwich bags so they don't get lost or mixed up and then laying out the whole thing on the towel on the bottom shelf of the cabinet. It's a big disassembled mess right now, but I can see a way forward: Cleaning it up and putting it back together with a new spark plug, then seeing if it starts. But I've got to tackle the carburetor before that.

Once the engine's in the cabinet, I stand and turn—and almost smack right into Nephi. Even with his own armful of parts and pieces—a glass tank, a plastic engine, some tools—he manages to duck back out of the way. The last thing I need is to deliver another head-butt, especially to him.

"Sorry," I say.

"Nice engine," he answers.

Those two words surprise me so much that I just stand there staring at him. Before I can snap out of it and respond, he motions toward the cabinet with his armful of stuff. "I've got to put this away," he says.

I step aside and head back to my seat in enemy territory.

The last thing I do before the bell rings is write down a list of parts I need so far. Now that I've read the book and had a good look at the engine, I think I have a decent idea what I need: a spark plug, carb cleaner, two-stroke engine oil, spray paint for the frame, maybe some new gaskets and diaphragms if they have them . . . It's small stuff. It's probably not a lot of money, but it's more than I have. *Where am I going to get the rest?* I think, but somewhere at the very bottom of my heart I'm pretty sure I already know.

I have this weird thought that people are like engines: We've got dark corners inside where the gunk collects too.

Gino and Dunk shoulder past me on the way out of the room. "You're dead meat, Freak," says Gino.

"Dead," echoes Dunk. "And you used like half of Rover's WD-40."

That was his? I didn't see his name on it, but he is making some big metal thing. So maybe I greased my way to the grave even more today, but I still feel like I got off to a good start on the engine. I just hope I live long enough to reach the finish line.

16

BUMPER BOWLING

SCHOOL IS OVER, and walkers are dismissed. We bumper-car our way through the crowded hallway toward the exit. A wintry mix has started up outside—sleet, freezing rain, maybe some hail. I can hear it slap and tick against the window, like it's waiting for me out there.

I see Nephi over at Maps's locker, and it kind of surprises me. How often do those two talk? About what? As I'm looking, Landrover slides up beside me. It's the end of the day, and I guess I just let my guard down. I'm cursing myself for not being more careful. But at first all he does is walk alongside me. "What d'you want?" I say. I'm trying to sound calm but will settle for anything less than terrified.

He slides closer and puts his arm around my shoulder. The nylon of his jacket slides against the nylon of mine. His arm comes to rest just above the curve in my upper back. We're walking slowly, his arm controlling my pace, my direction. It's a super-aggressive move but one that's completely invisible to the teachers. We pass right by Mrs. Gallego and she smiles. She's happy we seem to be getting along so well.

The hallway is loud but Landrover leans in. "You shouldn't have done that," he says.

"I didn't mean to—"

"And I heard something else too." I don't bother to ask what. I know he's going to tell me. "I heard you were giving my buds a hard time."

"What?" I say, honestly shocked. "That's not true. That is, like, the opposite of true."

"You calling them liars?" he says, wrenching me to a stop.

I stare down at my boots as the flow of kids breaks around us like a river around a rock. There is no right answer to that question.

"You think my name is funny?"

"No," I say, and I'm telling the truth too. I think his *nickname* is funny. I can see how being named after a luxury automobile might be a sore subject, though.

"Yeah you do," he says. "They told me."

I don't know what to say. It doesn't seem like clarifying the whole name/nickname thing is going to help, but I need to say something. All I manage to do is stammer out some half denials: "No . . . I . . . just . . . not your . . . name . . ."

He leans in close and whispers into my ear: "If I see you in maker space again, I'm going to have to *really* hurt you. Got it? Stay. *Away.*"

A chill drills right down to my core. His arm unlatches from my shoulder and he heads up the hallway, covering the short distance to the exit in big, confident strides. Landrover reaches the main door just as it's closing and punches it open with a two-hand shove. I hear the *ba-DOOOMP* echo through the hallway. It's a violent sound, and I flinch.

I lean against the wall and tell myself to breathe. This is bad. Landrover could slaughter me, and there wouldn't be anything I could do to stop him. He's big and fast and strong. He's a predator. And me? I'm prey. I'm playing the encounter over and over in my head, every part of it, everything I said and did that was wrong—but especially his threat.

I need maker space in order to fix the engine, but I can't go back. I'm stuck on this impossible puzzle as I leave school, and then—*OOF!* Someone bumps into me right before I reach the street. I brace myself, expecting to see Landrover again. Instead, two dark eyes glare out at me from under an overhang of black and purple hair, a black hood above that. Esme. It just feels unfair, like I'm being ganged up on.

"Watch where you're going," she says. *You bumped into me*, I want to say, but I don't. Even when it's true, it just ends up getting me pushed to the ground.

I expect her to keep going but she stands there, glaring at me.

"That engine's wrecked," she says. I have no idea why she cares. She's really angry and intimidating. I can't tell if she wants me to stay out of her way or is trying to start an argument. My head is buzzing like it's full of bees, and all I can think to say is: "Yeah, that's why I'm trying to fix it."

"So you can have a new toy?" she says, mocking me with a little-kid voice.

That's not fair. A little spark of anger scares off the bees. "No!" I say. "It's not even for me!"

It surprises her, either the words or the volume. For a second she just stares at me, but she recovers fast. "Good," she says. "You don't deserve it."

Deserve it? What does she mean by that? It doesn't even run. The little pellets of freezing rain are bouncing like fleas off the hood of her black parka. It's too old and too big for her, a hand-me-down. I can tell that she's poor too. You get a radar for that after a while. She's hiding under there, just like I do under my too-big clothes.

"Whatever," I mumble, just to say something. "I bought it."

She gives me a look like that's the most pathetic thing she's ever heard, then starts walking away. We're heading in the same direction now, but she's much faster. She levers away on her long legs like a midnight-black giraffe. Why did she want to talk about the engine? Or did she just want to insult me?

I shrug off my icy gear when I get home and go sit on the couch for a while. I don't turn on the Xbox or watch the TV or anything.

I just sit there trying to cool down and focus a little. I feel overheated and all over the place.

Ever since I found out about the bike it's been like bumper bowling. You know, where the ball just keeps careening down the lane, no matter how bad you rolled it? That's me, getting knocked around from all sides—Landrover, Esme, life—but still moving forward.

I finally get up off the couch, surprised that it's already so much darker out. I hunt around the apartment for the newspaper. It takes me a while, but I finally find it in the recycling. I pull it out and find the information about placing an ad yourself. Fixing the bike is only the first step. After that, I need to find someone to buy it. And it all has to happen before the twentieth.

NO SUCH THING AS FREE PIZZA

DAD DOESN'T GET HOME TILL SIX. That's late for him, and I'm starting to worry. He's gambling again. The dudes who take those bets—and collect them—are bad news. What if something has happened to him? It's a huge relief when I finally hear the key in the door. And it gets better. He flings the door open, smiling and carrying two pizza boxes. The smell of cheesy goodness fills the room, and I suddenly realize how hungry I am. "Two-for-one special!" he says.

"Sweet!" I say.

Listen, I know there are a hundred things going on right now and ninety-eight of them are bad. And I know maybe I should be handling all of this differently. Confronting Dad, confessing what I did, building a Landrover-proof suit out of scrap iron.

But one of the most important rules in life is this: Never question free pizza.

It's okay to be a little suspicious, though. Dad will definitely splurge on food sometimes: a surprise trip to the McDonald's drive-through or maybe we'll get ice cream in the summer. But he does that when things are going well. When he's got extra. But things are not going well right now—they're going off a cliff! And there are obviously better things to spend the money on. I *know* how short we are on rent money. In fact, I know even better than he does, since he doesn't know I took that money yet.

But maybe he knows something I don't too? Maybe the factory changed the rules about payday advances? Maybe he got the world's most unlikely raise? Maybe he had more of a plan than that ticket, and I won't need to make a big profit on this bike after all. I can feel the hope slipping in. "So," I say, my mouth full of melted cheese, "what's the occasion?"

I'm hoping he'll tip his hand and tell me something good. But he doesn't even look up, doesn't make eye contact. That worries me. I've seen that bad-dog body language from him way too many times. "St. Paddy's is coming up," he says between bites. "I guess it's just the luck of the Irish."

So that's it. Just his dumb bet, just the same superstitious nonsense it's always been with him. If he's already counting the imaginary money, I don't know why it should surprise me that he's already spending it. Dad's family is Irish from way back, and he probably thinks that makes this bet different, that his ancestors are practically rising up from the grave to hand him that ten thousand bucks.

I guess that's all the explanation I'm going to get, and really it's all I need. The hope leaks away. Sometimes I wish I didn't know him so well, which is a weird thing to wish about your dad.

It's amazing that we can eat an entire pizza while we're biting our tongues, but we do. We drink a whole two-liter bottle of Coke too. Afterward, Dad looks down at the empty bottle. "Wow, all that caffeine," he says. "I am never getting to sleep."

"Friday night, you can sleep in tomorrow," I say, even though he can sleep in every day.

"Woo-hoo!" says Dad, punching the air with his fist. Then he lets out a long, loud burp. I can't help it: I smile. It's been a while, and it feels good to feel good.

"Nice one," I say.

Normally this is when I'd retreat to my room, but not tonight. This is still our home. We're still here. It feels important to just, I don't know, *live here*—to squeeze something out of it. Anyway, whatever, after we clean up and put the second pizza in the fridge, I hand him the TV remote. "Your ship, Captain," I say, which is this thing we do.

We watch *SportsCenter* first. The season hasn't even started and the Red Sox big-money new free agent is already hurt. Dad tosses me the remote. "Take the wheel, Lieutenant."

I find *WALL-E*, just starting. I used to love this movie so hard. I look over to see if it's okay with Dad. He nods. "This is one of those kids' movies that's fun for adults too."

"I'm not a kid," I say. "I'm almost thirteen!"

He rolls his eyes and groans. "The terrible teens," he says.

"Yeah, I am going to have so many girls over," I say.

And then Dad comes up with one of his classic delayed comebacks. "Hey, if you're not a little kid, why did you choose this movie?"

I think about it and say, "Because it's fun for adults too."

He thinks that's pretty funny.

WALL-E is this little robot that's stranded on Earth all alone. Earth is abandoned and filled with junk, and he collects the best stuff out of it. Like he uses an old hubcap for a hat and does a little dance with it. It kind of reminds me of my Road Rokkit, just the idea of taking junk and making something good from it. I even wonder if that's where I got the idea. Not directly, but if I hadn't loved this movie so much when I was seven, would I be pinning so much on a total salvage job now?

I spend a lot of Saturday reading the engine book, going over the printouts, and planning things out in my head. I make it down to the library and burn most of my computer time watching YouTube videos on minibike repair. I can picture the engine lying there in pieces in that cabinet like a greasy Humpty Dumpty. It makes me so anxious I'm almost itchy. I can't make any mistakes putting it back together.

By Sunday, we're out of leftover pizza and I ride along as Dad drives downtown to Royston's. It's a quick, quiet car ride. It feels like our Friday-night truce is over and we're back to reality. The reality is: I'm keeping a huge secret from Dad, and he thinks he's keeping a huge secret from me. The one good thing about all this guilt and worry is that I think it's helping me understand Dad a little better—at least why he's so quiet most of the time.

Dad pushes the cart at the store and he's annoyed the whole time because it has one bad wheel up front. It doesn't roll as much as lurch. I know how much stuff I'm allowed to put in the cart at this point. He gives me the evil eye on the Peanut Butter Cap'n Crunch—not because it's bad for me but because it's expensive.

"Most important meal of the day!" I say, and he gives in. Normally I'd consider that a straight-up victory, but now I'm wondering—did I convince him, or is he just spending more of that imaginary leprechaun money?

Afterward, we put our bags in the back seat. I start to climb in the front, but he says, "Let's go look at the tower."

His pot of gold, I think. We size up the weather as we walk. There's no leprechaun-style rainbow, but it's the first decent day in a while. It's definitely above freezing now, with the late-morning sun beating straight down on us. The patches of dirt and grass are growing, and the snow that's left has a wet shimmer to it.

I can see Dad eyeing it nervously. It has to warm up like this if that tower is going to fall, but it can't warm up *too* much. He's still got almost a week to go.

"Are your tickets, like, soon?" I say, all fake innocent. I'm baiting him again, trying to get him to tell me something. He doesn't bite.

"Don't jinx it," he says.

Still poking: "It would be awesome if you won."

He just nods. Silent.

I look around at the sun, the grass, the water dripping steadily from the roofs and branches. My ticket is for the same day as Dad's bookie bet, just later. March 17, nine p.m. In a weird way, it seems like teamwork. But unlike him, I know better than to start counting the money. The whole reason my ticket is for nine p.m. is because it was the earliest one left on that day. No one wants nine p.m. That's nighttime, when the sun is long gone and the pond is probably starting to refreeze. I just got that ticket to be part of the contest. To be part of something. It's a stupid bet, but if you've been listening, you know what I'm going to say next:

All. Bets. Are. Stupid.

We're walking really slowly, and that's annoying Dad even more. The Presbyterian church just let out, and the sidewalk is full of people dressed nicer than us. When Mom was still around, we used to go to church a few times a year: Christmas and Easter and things like that. I haven't been since she left. Neither has Dad—not even to Our Lady of the Horse Track.

"Look at all these Holy Rollers," he says under his breath. He cuts around a big family and I have to step off the sidewalk to follow him. I can feel the wet snow through the hole in my sneaker.

The "Thin Ice Days" banner is up at the entrance to the park. This is where the band concert will be, if the weather's nice enough. It's less than a week away now. We stop walking, and Dad stares across the ice at the tower. He's looking at it the way a hungry dog looks at a steak. His poker face falls away, and all I see there now is desperation.

I don't like seeing Dad like this, so I look over at the tower. The ice beneath it is slick and shiny in the sun. It looks like it could fall in right now.

I hope Dad wins—or I do—but I already know deep down that we won't.

More people come in. The Catholic church must have let out too. The Catholics dress a little more formally. I see black pants and white shirts and little girls in pastel dresses. But I also see missing buttons and fabric worn so thin it's shiny. I see a baby stroller with a busted wheel, lurching along just like our shopping cart. The baby inside isn't even bothering to cry. It's amazing how much you can get used to, and how fast.

The church bells are ringing as I take one last look around. I wonder if it's just a Sunday stroll for these people, or if they're checking on their tickets too. *They all look like they could really use the money*, I think, but that's wrong. That's thinking like Dad again. I correct myself: *They all look like they have better things to spend those three dollars on.*

18

BOXED OUT

LANDROVER IS COMING at me like a missile before second period on Monday, and I'm caught out in the open in a half-empty hallway. I look around for a teacher or trapdoor or any other form of escape. What I see is Maps coming up behind me. We haven't really talked in a long time, but Landrover is closing in fast and, well, here goes nothing. I turn.

"BAMF!" I say. Maps collects old X-Men comics, and that's the sound Nightcrawler makes when he teleports, disappearing one place and appearing somewhere else. It kind of means "Get me out of here!" to us—at least it used to.

Maps sort of smiles, but he keeps walking. Then he spots Landrover and his eyes narrow. "SNIKT!" he says. It's the noise Wolverine's claws make when they pop out of his hands. He stops next to me.

"S'up," he says to Landrover as he gets closer. Landrover just nods and keeps walking. And that's it, the whole encounter. But you know what? It's enough.

Maps walks away in his Celtics jersey and crew cut and Jordans, and it takes me a second to figure out what it reminds me of. It's that stupid book, how I hate the way everyone is just one thing. Because Maps looks like the biggest, squarest jock on the planet, but we just had a conversation 100 percent in vintage comic book slang.

I manage to avoid Landrover the rest of the morning, but things get a lot more complicated at the start of lunch.

"Where my makers?" calls Mr. Feig.

I hesitate, or my feet do, anyway. They just refuse to move. I thought about this all weekend and still haven't come up with a solution. I need to get to maker space to keep working on my engine, but I'm terrified to cross Landrover again. I'm doomed either way.

I watch Nephi step out of the lunch line, then Landrover, Gino, Haley, Dunk, Joe, and a bunch of guys I don't remember seeing there before. I picture the engine, lying in pieces on that towel. I remember the rent box, the feel of those bills, and I know nothing Landrover can do to me could be worse. I guess that's what does it, because I finally step forward to join them.

Or I try to, anyway, because the kid behind me in line gives me an absolutely perfect flat tire. He steps on the back of my sneaker just as I'm lifting it from the ground and the whole shoe nearly comes off.

I look back to see who did it. It's this guy named Mark who I barely even know. Why would he do that?

"Hey, Freak," I hear. It's Haley. "Are your shoes on sale?"

I feel my ears begin to get hot, my face begin to flush. There's duct tape patching the hole in the bottom and for a second I'm afraid she can see it. "No!" I say.

"Really?" she says. "Because they're half-off."

Everyone around me in the line busts out laughing.

I just stand there with my mouth open. I'm trying to think of a comeback, but my mind is just one big buzzing blank again.

"Brutal!" someone cheers.

I look at Mark, like: Why? He just smiles at me as I bend down to fix my sneaker. My back rounds even more, and I know everyone is watching.

And then I get it. Mark's friends with Landrover. He just did that to stall me.

I wrestle my shoe back on and hustle to catch up to the group, but I'm too late. The line is already disappearing around the corner, and no one is going to let me cut. All the regular kids are at the front, and there's a string of new ones at the back. I size them up. They are size Large, even Extra Large. Jocks, kids with money—Landrover's friends. He's brought more than enough to fill the room.

I'm boxed out.

Mr. Feig gives me a look—sad or tired or maybe both—and then swings the door closed on the two of us who didn't make the sign-in sheet. I look at Mark. I hear he's good at baseball. "Bummer," he says happily.

He walks away, but I just stand there for a while looking at the closed door. My engine is in there, and I'm not. Landrover said he was really going to hurt me, and I've got to hand it to him. This one really hurts.

AFTER HOURS

LANDROVER HAS ME BOXED out of maker space, and I'm sure he's going to keep it that way. He probably likes having his friends in there anyway. It's a major problem, and I hover around after science class to talk to Mr. Feig about it. I don't know what I'm going to say. I don't want to be a snitch or a sneak or a teacher's pet or anything like that, but I need to say *something*. I have to get back in there!

Feig takes one look at me, standing there by the door like a slice of lunch meat someone threw against the wall, and says, "Ked, my man. Come with me."

"Okay," I say and follow him out the door.

"I have to run down to the office," he says, answering my question before I ask it. "But we can walk and talk. I think I know what this is about."

"I need to get into maker space . . . tomorrow," I say. "I have to work on my engine."

"I'm kind of in a pickle," he says. "There's a limit on how many kids we can have in there. It's not safe if it's too crowded. You gotta get there before the sheet fills up. I can't play favorites."

"I tried," I say.

"Oh yeah?"

Now he turns so his glasses square me up, but I don't want to tell on Mark. He'd just claim it was an accident anyway. I try something else. "Those new guys today, they aren't really makers, are they?"

I'm not sure what a "real maker" is. I just started going myself. Mr. Feig smiles as we walk down the crowded hallway, dodging bodies and backpacks. "Sure they're makers," he says. "Troublemakers."

Now I smile. "Ha-ha. Yeah."

We turn a corner. This hallway is less crowded, and he stops. I stop too. "Listen, I think I might have a solution to our"—he pauses, searching for the right phrase—"overflow issue."

I look up at this human stovepipe with glasses and wonder how much he knows about what's going on, how much he sees.

"Oh yeah?" I say. "What kind of solution?"

"You have any time after school?"

"I've got nothing but."

He nods. "Well, I've got a mountain of work for these new tests we've got coming up. I usually stay after school, at least an hour or two. There's always too much to do."

"Okay . . ." I say, not really sure where he's going with this.

"So I can correct tests in maker space, and you can work on your bike."

"I like it," I say. "I like it a lot."

"We can start today if you like," he says.

The warning bell goes off. "I'm going to be late," I say, but I say it through this huge smile I just can't get off my face.

So school ends, but I stay. It's a strange feeling. I'm not big on "extracurricular activities." I mean, you've seen how my school days have been going, right? Why would I sign up for more of that?

But here I am: technically allowed to go home but pushing open the door to the library instead. I'll be honest: I'm a little nervous. I trust Mr. Feig, I'm just wondering what the catch is. I've learned that when adults do something nice for you, there's almost always a catch—like when Mom bought me that Xbox and then left for Oregon.

I squeeze inside the maker space door. Mr. Feig is bent like a noodle over a stack of printouts. He looks up and blinks at me through his thick lenses, but I can tell his eyes are still focused two feet ahead and not really seeing me.

"Cabinet's open," he says, already looking down at the papers again.

I look over toward the cabinet and see someone else sitting on the far side of the table. She's so quiet and still that I didn't even notice her at first.

Oh no.

It's Esme.

I'm so surprised to see her that I do that thing where you, like, twitch. It's like a double take for my whole body, a single big shiver. And then I just stand there staring.

"Yes?" she says, looking up from her model. She's all in black and she's holding a scary-looking X-Acto knife in her right hand. Her purple hair is in her eyes a little but she blows it expertly to the side with a puff of air. I push my hair back too.

"I'm going to go to the cabinet."

"Knock yourself out," she says, and I get the feeling she means it literally. What is her problem with me?

I look back at Mr. Feig, but he's still bent over his papers, fully focused. He could've mentioned I'd be sharing the room with a knife-wielding eighth-grade goth girl who hates me.

She goes back to work and I decide to do the same. I figure I'll be okay with Mr. Feig a few chairs away. Still better than Landrover, I tell myself, as I drop my stuff on the table and head over to the open cabinet.

I spend some time cleaning the parts. Then I check them out one by one: turning gears, pressing levers, checking connections. There's no major damage, nothing split or bent, no broken parts to add to my shopping list. I put the engine back together slowly and carefully. It takes a lot of concentration and memory, but it's surprisingly straightforward too. Every piece has a place, and it's all the exact opposite of how I took it apart. For a second I can't find the last bolt I need to put the crankcase back on, and I panic. Then I realize it slid under the edge of the towel. I see it hiding under there like a fuzzy lump.

Once I fasten the last bolt, I step back. Now I'm the one blinking and trying to refocus my eyes. The reassembled engine gleams up at me. There are a few little dents here and there, a few nicks in the middle, but it's all on the surface. Everything inside is clean and in the right place—at least as near as I can tell from the book and the diagrams and the fact that the screws fit. This section of the engine should work. So why doesn't it run? Maybe it was the gunk, maybe it's the old spark plug. More likely . . .

I look over at the carburetor. That's the next step. It's the fuel injection system, and there is zero chance it's not pretty clogged up too. The guy told me the engine wasn't working, and a gunked-up carburetor seems like an obvious suspect.

But it's not sturdy like the rest of the engine. The parts in that were solid enough to just pull out and clean. The carb has a lot of small, tricky pieces. In the YouTube videos some of them look about as fragile as wet paper. Taking them out and cleaning them will be like open-heart surgery. And if I mess up, even once . . .

"Mr. Feig?" says Esme, sort of snapping me out of it.

"Esme, you know I can't help you with your model," he says. "The contest . . ."

"Yeah, I know," she says flatly. "You'd need a sense of style for that."

Ouch, but it's true. Mr. Feig almost always looks like he got dressed in the dark. I look over to see how he'll take it. Will she get in trouble? Instead, he barks out a laugh. Esme cracks a smile and says, "Never mind. I figured it out." I look back and forth between them. Wait, these two joke around? It surprises me, and sort of makes me wonder if I know anything about either of them.

I look back at my stuff and see the fuel tank and hoses I detached from the engine at the start. Those are big, solid parts that even an idiot like me can handle. So I get to work on them: cleaning, reconnecting, tightening. I even use some more of the WD-40. (What? His name's not on it.)

Just as I reconnect the main hose, Mr. Feig stands up and begins collecting his stuff. The timing is so perfect that I wonder if he was waiting for me.

"That's all, folks," he says.

I stay on my side of the table and let Esme put her stuff away first. I have to admit her model is pretty cool: a tightly packed little city of black roofs and spires. It reminds me of something from *The Lord of the Rings*. But then I see the way it's divided by one main street, the way the buildings get a little taller at the center, and I realize I'm looking at downtown Norton—or at least some futuristic version of it.

Once she puts all her sharp angles and edges away, it's my turn. I eye the carburetor. I need to tackle that tomorrow or I'll run out of time. I still have to get the actual frame fixed up, reconnect the engine, and test it all. My heart is racing just thinking about it as I slide the engine onto the shelf for another night.

As I begin to back up, I bump into something. I spin around. Esme is standing right behind me. I flinch, afraid she's going to hit me or push me. But she's not even looking at me. She's looking down at the engine. Staring down at it, really. She snaps out of it when she sees me looking and leaves without another word.

I don't get her fixation with this engine. I mean, yeah, the bikes are cool in the videos. In another life maybe I'd like to fix this one up just to keep it and ride it around the trails outside town. But I don't understand why she seems so mad at me for having it now. The engine is lying in sections on a towel like a peeled orange. It's a total work in progress. I guess maybe we all are, though.

SPY MISSION

I NEED TO GET THE PARTS and fuel for the bike. That means I need to go to Landrover's dad's store, the only auto parts store in town. I know for a fact that Landrover works there after school sometimes. I've seen him. And if you think running into him during school is bad news, imagine him with no teachers around. I also need more money for this. That's not good either. I have to do hard things now, and my plan is to get through this like a spy. No, like an *assassin*. All action, all forward momentum. No second thoughts.

First, I head straight home. Head down, I motor. I do what I came to do. No, what I *need* to do. Then I rest, but just a little. I sit down on the couch because I was standing for most of the time I was working on the engine—and all of the way home, obviously.

I ease my upper back into the old, body-battered cushion.

Like my dad says, I take a load off. Five minutes, ten, then I'm up and out the door. Assassin!

I head straight for the auto parts store. I proceed with caution. Spy. I look around carefully when I enter, wincing as the bell above the door gives me away. I don't see Landrover anywhere—and he's taller than the shelves, so I would.

I relax a little and find the spark plug I need right away. Then I grab a plastic bottle of two-stroke engine oil. There are a few different kinds of carb cleaner. I take a small can of the cheapest. I find the big case of spray paint easily too, but it's locked. I ask the man behind the counter. Landrover's dad. He decides I don't look like a graffiti artist or glue huffer. He gets out from behind the counter slowly. He's a big man.

I want a basic black and a classic fire-engine red to match what's left of the bike's original color.

"Which brand?" he says.

"The cheapest."

He gives me a sour look, and since I'm already annoying him, I ask my next question: "Do you have gaskets and diaphragms and stuff for a minibike?"

The string of engine terms seems to snap him back into customer service mode. "I could probably order them for you if you know the make and model," he says.

"They don't make these bikes anymore," I say. I figure that's that. It was a long shot anyway, but he keeps talking. "A lot of the engines are pretty similar. You know how many cc we're talking?"

And believe it or not I do: cc means cubic centimeters. Not to get too technical about it, but it's a way to measure engine capacity. "Forty nine," I say. I know a lot about the engine by now.

"Let me check," he says, disappearing into the back room as I get the rest of the things on my list. I check and double-check the prices. I do the math in my head.

Landrover's dad is waiting for me once I reach the register. "All I got," he says, sliding a plastic baggie across the counter. I pick it up. There's a layer of dust on the front. Inside is an assortment of thin black shapes, like construction paper cutouts. I read the faded label, some brand I've never heard of. "Gasket set for 2-stroke 43cc mini dirt bike engine. May also fit some 49cc and 47cc models."

May, I think, *I always liked that month.* "How much?"

"I can let you have it for five bucks." This thing has been gathering dust in his back room for years, but I'm not in a great position to negotiate.

I take the bills out of my pocket. The same bills I just took out of the box at home. I unfold them carefully and hand them over. I only get a few singles back. *No second thoughts,* I tell myself. Assassin.

I go straight home and get the number I wrote down for the paper. Then I get my language arts notebook, where I wrote down what I want my ad to say. The paper charges by the character, so I wrote it down in the same part where I wrote my haiku poem assignment. Those have to be short too: 5-7-5.

My ad says:

"Vintage ROAD ROKKIT! Good condition. Runs great. $600 OBO." Then I give my number and say, all in caps, "CALL BTW 2–5 ONLY!!!"

It's not a haiku. "OBO" means "Or Best Offer." I look it over and add one thing. New paint. Nine characters. I change it to Nu paint, but I keep it. You've got to spend money to make money.

I tried to place this ad online at the library, but that requires a credit card number. So now I pick up the phone and take a deep breath. An old lady answers. She's super friendly, and I tell her what I want the ad to say. "It has to go in *this week's* paper," I add. "Online too. *This* week."

"That's not a problem," she says.

Phew!

"And how will you be paying?"

That might be a problem. I close my eyes. "Do you take checks?"

"Are you old enough to have checks?" Her voice is as warm as a bowl of mac and cheese but she sounds skeptical.

"I'll have my dad mail it."

She pauses. I hold my breath.

"You seem like a very serious young man," she says finally. "I can make an exception."

"Great!" I say before she can change her mind. "He'll mail it tomorrow."

My dad is always mailing imaginary checks. I feel a little bad about lying, but it's okay. By the time they realize the check isn't there, I'll have the money. I can just walk it down to their office.

When Dad comes home, I act normal. I think he's trying to do the same thing. We talk about the weather without ever quite mentioning the tower. It's warm again today, but not too warm. Below freezing tonight, they say. All in all, he seems pleased—he likes his chances. He actually thinks his bet will pay off. I hope one of ours does.

A BIG BUT

I SLIP INTO SCHOOL on Tuesday with my new supplies rattling around in my backpack. I stash them in my locker and all day long I feel like I've got a secret. I keep my distance when I pass Landrover in the hallway, but I'm smiling to myself. *You didn't beat me.*

Steering clear of him means steering clear of maker space during the day. (If going was even an option, stuffed full of his jerk friends.) I think it's okay, though. Fingers crossed, I should have everything I need to finish the engine now, and the rest of the bike isn't so bad. The wheels are still holding air, and they seem to roll and stop fine. The frame needs to be straightened out in a few places and repainted, but that seems pretty straightforward.

The paper comes out Wednesday, and I figure a buyer will contact me right away—I mean, it's a Road Rokkit. (Okay, maybe "hope" is a better word than "figure." Okay, maybe "pray.") But that would still mean selling it Thursday or Friday at the earliest. That's cutting it close on the rent. And I still have to get everything put back together and running. But—and this is a BIG BUT—I'm starting to see a way that this could all work. So, yeah, I'll steer clear of Landrover. None of this works if I'm dead.

Of course, not being in the maker space during the day means I'm back in the caf at lunch. And that's nothing to smile about. I radar-scan the room as I navigate my tray to that same empty table in the back corner. I got the hot lunch today—reduced price, but not free.

At least the back corner's a good perch to watch the action. I see a flash of purple float by: Esme. She lands at a table half-full of eighth-grade girls. Everyone's more popular than me. But if she's in here, then she's not in maker space either. Just after school. *Is it just Landrover's friends taking up the spots,* I wonder, *or is it something else?*

I see Danny with his new crew, and Maps with a table of jock royalty—it's like the Knights of the Round Table but for basketball. Maps saved my bacon yesterday, but he still feels so far away most of the time, like I'm looking up at him from the bottom of a lake. I walked by him this morning, and I was going to say hi. Just hi, that's it. But he was surrounded by his super-cool friends like usual. Surrounded by guys who don't even know I exist. So I just kept my head down and walked by.

I move on to the weirdly powdery chocolate pudding. The truth is, when I imagine my life here how I want it to be, when I just let my mind go for it and picture myself happy and surrounded by friends, it's not new friends. It's those guys again: Nephi, Danny, and Maps. Maybe that's pathetic—I don't know.

I do know this: When I look over at Danny and Maps, I don't see them laughing much. Most of the time, they're not even talking—just nodding and listening. It doesn't prove anything. For all I know, they crack up the second I look away. But it's weird. Back when we sat together, we used to talk and laugh all the time. We'd talk over each other and laugh until food was flying out of our mouths—then we'd laugh at that. We'd bet our Tater Tots like poker chips, Danny always the first to go all in. Nephi cautious, betting one tot at a time.

Maybe it's because they're mostly the new guys in new groups. I'm sure they'll figure it out. They've got time—and they've got friends. That's the important thing.

I'm still thinking about all those things after lunch: new friends, old friends, walking by Maps this morning. And that's when I turn the corner on my way to my locker and nearly crash into Nephi. And I guess that's why I say what I do.

"Hey, Neff."

Neff does the last thing in the world I expect him to. He stops.

"Hey, Ked."

Not Freakins, not Freak. Ked. And you know how it is when someone who really knows you calls you by your name? How it has a different feel to it? Well, that. Maybe even better than normal because these days I feel like I barely even know myself, like I'm a caterpillar in a cocoon going: *What the heck is even happening to me?* And I want to keep the old familiar feeling going, so I keep talking.

"How was maker space?" I say.

Nephi looks at me for a second. I'm afraid he's just going to say "fine" or something like that and keep walking, but he surprises me again. He steps off to the side of the busy hallway to make space to talk. I step there with him.

"It was good. I made some progress," he says. "Someone was using the screwdriver I needed but I just worked on something else." Then he seems to realize something and he hesitates. "Why weren't you there?"

"Well," I say, "that's what I wanted to talk to you about."

Is it? I guess so.

"Oh, yes?" he says as I try to shuffle my words into some kind of order.

"Yeah," I say. "Feig let me stay after school to work on my engine. He has the room open."

"Oh, yes?" he says again. It's such a Nephi thing to say too: a formal attempt to be casual. He seems interested.

"Yeah, it's kind of cool. It's like private maker space. No . . . distractions."

"Landrover's friends are the worst," he says, knowing what I mean. "They make it hard to concentrate."

"You should come by today," I say. "After school, I mean. If you want." This feels like spending money I don't have too. I don't know if I can even make this offer. I just know that I want to. So I do.

PROGRESS

IN THE LIBRARY DURING study hall, I rewatch a YouTube video on taking apart and cleaning a minibike carburetor. It's not a Road Rokkit, but the carb looks pretty similar. And here's the thing: The video is only ten minutes long. I mean, yeah, the guy is a professional mechanic, but still: This is doable.

As soon as school ends I head straight for maker space. I head up the hill as all the little kids are heading down it. I feel like a salmon swimming past sunfish. I think I'm doing a pretty good job of it, but Esme blows by me like I'm standing still. She's taller and purpler, and the little kids get out of her way.

When I get to maker space, she's already in her spot, bent over the black plastic spires of her model with the hot glue gun in one hand. She doesn't even look up, but at least Mr. Feig gives me a smile.

I drop my bag of supplies at the same seat as yesterday and go over to the cabinet. I get my stuff and one of the pairs of safety goggles, because carb cleaner is no joke.

126

I spread everything out on the table. I replay the YouTube video in my head and put the little gasket kit and the other stuff I'm going to need in a little cluster on my right. I position the carburetor in the center of the towel. It sits there: dense, delicate, the heart of the engine. I'm pretty sure the problem with the engine is somewhere inside. I slide the goggles over my eyes, pick up the can of carb cleaner, and put my finger on the button. Here goes absolutely everything . . .

"Uh, knock knock?"

We all look over toward the half-open door. It's Nephi. It feels good to see him. He was my friend for so long and I don't know what we are now, exactly, but he's here. I invited him and he came. It feels like, I don't know, something.

"Who's there?" says Mr. Feig.

"It's me, Nephi."

I smile. He's so literal.

"I can see that," says Mr. Feig.

Nephi gives him a look, like: *Then why did you ask?*

Mr. Feig doesn't even ask Nephi why he came or who told him about it, which is a major relief. He just says, "Welcome aboard," like this is a cruise ship or something.

"All right," says Nephi as he walks into the room and straight over to the cabinet.

I'm about to get back to work when I hear: "Ked, could you help me with this?" It's Nephi. He's crouched down, peering into one of the lower shelves of the cabinet. "It's caught on something, and I don't want to break it."

"Sure, sure," I say, getting up and heading toward the cabinet.

The biggest piece of his model is a glass tank, like a fish tank. The other parts seem to be stashed inside. We each get on one side, reach into the cabinet, and try to slide it out. It moves like an inch and that's it. "Yeah, it's stuck," I say.

We both lean in to try to see what, but it's dark back there. Suddenly—*bump*—we're both pushed out of the way by someone coming up right between us. "Get your stubby seventh-grade arms out of the way," she says. It's Esme. She reaches into the cabinet, fishes around a little, and then slides the tank out smoothly.

"Thanks, S," says Nephi as she puts the tank on the table. *S?* I think. I guess they know each other from maker space. It shouldn't surprise me, but it does.

"I'm sorry those guys were giving you a hard time," he says, keeping his voice low.

"Typical dude-bros," she says with a casual shrug that I don't believe. Right away I think of Landrover's friends who invaded maker space. I remember what Mr. Feig said about them: *Sure they're makers. Troublemakers.* Time on their hands and a purple-haired girl to pester—I guess that's why she's not in there during the day anymore either. Mr. Feig invited both of us to this space. He found a way to make room for everyone. But he also handed regular maker space over to the barbarian hordes.

"What am I looking at, Neff?" I say, because, I'll be honest, I'm feeling a little left out.

Nephi looks over at me. I'm on the opposite side of him from Esme. I feel like she did that on purpose, but the three of us are still standing around, and she's not glaring at me. It feels like progress.

Nephi picks up a sign, hand-painted but precise: "Renewable River Power for the Twenty-First Century."

"Okay," I say.

"This is a water turbine," he says, holding up a plastic case. There's a metal rod coming out of one end with a little plastic propeller on it.

"So you fill this tank with water, the water spins that propeller, and . . . it generates electricity?" I say.

"Exactly," he says.

"But how do you get the water to move?"

He points to the small electric engine I saw him working on the other day.

"Oh yeah," I say. "That's pretty awesome." I mean it too. The design is impressive, and the river is what makes Norton special. It's why the town is here, why the factory is. "I hope you win," I say.

"Fehh," says Esme. So much for progress.

We all get down to business after that. I start with the can of carb cleaner. I go over every inch of the carburetor, turning the greasy block with my fingers like a rotisserie chicken. *PSST! PSST! PSST!*

I dry off the metal and pick up the screwdriver. For such small bikes, Road Rokkits have pretty complex carburetors. I take off the bottom cover first, and the first thing I see is the metering diaphragm. It's made of thin synthetic rubber, and I am terrified it is going to come apart in my hands when I try to remove it. I pinch the edge softly and begin peeling it away slowly—so so so slowly. I feel little pinpricks on my forehead as the nervous sweat begins to push its way to the surface.

Finally, it comes free. Somehow, miraculously, it is still in one piece. I set it aside. It feels like that one piece alone took as long as the whole YouTube video. I lean in and keep going, arranging the parts in the same order I remove them in so I'll know how to put them back.

The metal parts aren't so bad, even the little springs and pins. I go as slowly and gently as I can, cleaning as I go, sometimes blasting away with the spray can and sometimes dabbing away delicately with a balled-up tissue.

Now that I'm inside the carburetor, it's pretty obvious that the engine wouldn't have run the way it was. It was a lot more gunked up than the one in the video. I'm pretty sure this was the problem with the engine, and it's a relief to find it. But I'm not done yet, and trying to peel an intake gasket free, my miracles run out. The thing comes apart in my hands.

I groan softly and sit back. Disaster. I open and close my fingers to let them uncramp. I pick up the little five-dollar repair kit I got at the shop. Wrong model, wrong cc, but it's my only chance. I reread the part on the label that says "may fit" 49cc engines. I feel a little better, and I find a piece that more or less matches the one I just shredded.

The new material is a little thinner, more like heavy paper than rubber, but the shape is . . . close. Maybe I can make this work? I look across the table. "Uh, Esme?" I say. "Can I borrow that X-Acto knife for a sec?"

I must look pretty pathetic, my hands greasy and my eyes needy, because the look she gives me is more sad than annoyed. She puts down the knife she's holding and picks up a different one. "You can borrow this old one," she says. "The blade's kind of dull anyways."

She pulls back her hand like she's going to toss it. "That's okay!" I blurt, raising my hands in front of me. "I'll come get it."

I push the torn, old gasket back together and lay it on top of the new one. Then I just kind of trace the shape. The so-called dull razor on the end of the knife cuts through the thin material easily. It's not a perfect match, but it's not bad. I'm still worried, though. The videos didn't mention anything about this.

Esme clears her throat in that attention-getting way. I look up to see what she wants. "Uh, *my knife?*" she says in a tone generally reserved for infants and small mammals.

Is she serious? She wasn't even using this one?

"You can't just have all my stuff," she says.

She's serious. I feel like rolling it across the table at her, but Mr. Feig is watching now—and it does have a pointy razor blade on the end. I get up again and walk it back around the table. I ignore how annoyed I am and say, "Thanks."

Sure she spoke to me like a gerbil, but she helped me out too.

She considers it for a second, then gives the tiniest of nods. "It's okay." When I'm halfway back to my seat she adds: "Let me know if you need the sharp one."

That is literally the nicest thing she's ever said to me, and when I sit back down, I manage to take apart the rest of the carb without tearing anything else with my fat fingers.

More progress. I'll take it.

THE LATE SHIFT

MR. FEIG CLEARS HIS THROAT. I think he's ready to go.

"Mr. Feig," I say, "can I have a little more time?"

"You're killin' me, Eakins!" he says, but you can tell he's joking.

I don't want to leave the carburetor in pieces like this, so I start putting it back together. I'm not saying it's ten minutes, but it's a lot faster than before. All I have to do is the reverse of what I just did, putting the screws I took out back in and stuff like that. There's a little pinching and pushing to make the new gasket fit, but not too much.

Mr. Feig is watching, and as I put the cover back on and tighten the last screw he starts putting his papers away. Nephi pretends he doesn't notice and keeps working, but Esme starts gathering up her stuff. After all that tense, silent work, I feel like talking to someone.

"Why's your whole town painted black anyway?" I say.

I'm afraid she's not going to answer, but she answers right away. In fact, she answers so fast that I almost wonder if she was waiting for someone to ask her that.

"It's photovoltaic paint," she says. "I mean, it's not really. That technology doesn't exist yet. But that's what it's supposed to be."

Nephi finally stops what he's doing and looks over. He has needle-nose pliers in one hand and a wire in the other. "Photovoltaic," he says. "That's good. Every inch of surface area would become a solar cell. Hypothetically."

"That's really cool," I say.

Esme is so happy she nearly smiles. "Plus," she adds, "the enemy will have a harder time seeing it at night."

Nephi nods very seriously.

"Of course," I say.

We've been silent this whole time but suddenly the dam has burst. Nephi points to a wire trailing down the side of one of the buildings in Esme's model. "What's that?" he asks.

"That connects to this," she says, pointing to the little roof. "See? A real solar cell. It's like an example of what the paint would do."

"Nice," he says. "What does it power?"

"That's what I'm trying to figure out," she says. "I was thinking, like, a streetlight. But then I was thinking it might be weird to have just one."

I've been kind of hovering on the outside of the conversation, but I've also been scanning her model. I know downtown really well from my walks. I take a step closer and point at a square building right in the center of Main Street. "This is the bank, right?"

She hesitates for just a second before answering: "Yeah, so?"

"Well, if you . . . I mean . . ." She gives me a look like, *Spit it out already*, and I finally do. "You know how there's that big display out front with the time and temperature?"

"That's a good idea," says Nephi. "You could move the solar cell over to this roof . . ."

"Oh, yeah!" says Esme, warming up to the idea. "Then bring the wire down here—you wouldn't even see it—and all I need is like an old digital watch to take apart. Then I can put a solar-powered bank clock right on Main Street." She pauses, thinking about it. "I mean, they'll still have time in the future."

"The future *is* time," says Nephi, and it basically blows all of our minds.

"Whoooa," I say.

Mr. Feig brings us back to reality. "Okay, seriously, I like the enthusiasm, but I have got to go."

I check out Nephi's model as he puts his stuff away. It's a legit hydroturbine and he's going to fill the tank with water when he's done. It seems amazing to me. I'm rebuilding something from videos and guides and printouts. Neff and Esme are building something out of thin air. *Where do they get these ideas?* I think. But then I realize I just gave Esme an idea too. I get that feeling again, that feeling of being a part of something.

With the carburetor back together and nothing to do but pick up my stuff, I can finally really think about what they're doing, about what the contest means. Building a Better Norton . . . They're picturing it in their heads—what that means, what it might look like—and then they're making those ideas real.

We stand up one by one and slide our stuff back into the cabinet. My engine is almost done. Hopefully tomorrow I can reattach it to the frame. Then I'll see if it starts, maybe even take it out for a test drive. The paper comes out with my ad tomorrow too. Things are happening, moving forward.

"This is good," says Nephi to no one in particular as he slides his tank inside the cabinet. "You can get a lot of work done in here when it's quiet like this."

"We're like the late shift," I say, because both our dads work half-time at the factory.

"The late shift," he repeats. "I like it."

"You two can be the late shift," says Esme. "I'll be the great shift."

Nephi waves her off, like, *Oh, please*, but I don't argue.

We split up like usual once we get outside, with Mr. Feig heading for his car and Esme's long, eighth-grade limbs giving her an instant lead. But so much has happened today—and some of it was even good. I'm starting to think: *Maybe things don't have to be like usual.*

"Hey, Neff," I say. "Wait up."

HARD TRUTHS, COLD FACTS

NEPHI LOOKS BACK. I hustle to catch up.

"What's up?" he says, all business.

And this might sound stupid, but I don't really have a what's up. There's nothing I want to talk to him about, in particular. It's just that he was there and I was there and we were all talking, even joking. I mean, he showed me his tank! I thought we'd just hang and walk together for a while until we had to split up. It's a cold day, but the sky is no more gray than usual and we've got our jackets. It's not head-down-and-hustle-home weather.

But those two words, and the way he said them, let me know he's not thinking the same thing. And I guess that just makes me mad. "You're welcome," I say.

"What?" he says.

"For telling you about the extra maker space."

He looks at me carefully. "What's your problem?" he says.

"I guess you can hang out with me when no one else is there to see it, huh?"

"We weren't alone," he says, literal again.

"Oh yeah, Esme—excuse me, *S!*—your best bud!"

"I don't even really know her," he says. "She's just nice."

That statement is a lot less shocking to me now than it would have been yesterday, but I don't want to get into it. "Yeah?" I say. "How about you?"

He opens his mouth to say something but he doesn't even get the chance. Here it comes. I can feel it all boiling up inside me. It's like that moment when you know you're going to throw up and all you can do is rush to get to the toilet in time. "I don't even know why I'm surprised! Of course you'd ditch me again. Just like you ditched me before. Just like you all did!"

And now it's not even about him anymore, or not about just him, but he's the only one here now. The word vomit continues: about lunch, about school. I think I mention the lake at some point. It's honestly a bit of a blur.

"Ked!" says Nephi. "Shut up." I stop, out of breath anyway.

"You're the one who stopped coming to the lake," he says.

"I was embarrassed!" I shout. It surprises both of us. It's the first time I've said it out loud, but of course it's true. They didn't ask me to stop coming, weren't mean to me, didn't freeze me out . . . I stopped showing up. Was that it, the beginning of the end for us?

I probably look like a maniac, red-faced and shouting and

waving my arms, but Nephi is calm. Even though I was shouting in his face. What he says next, he says softly.

"And you lied to us."

"What do you . . ." I begin, but something stops me.

"Taking up running?" he says. "How's that going?"

Oh, I think. *That. But that was . . .*

Nephi starts walking again, but I stay planted. The cold wind cools my overheated face. I always thought that Maps left the group first. At least, that's what I always told myself. But it's not true. I guess *I* did. I'm seeing it through their eyes now. After all the hours I've spent thinking about this, this is the first time I've looked at it from the other side.

I watch Nephi walk away, the wind whipping his khaki pants. It was me. I broke the trust. I left the group. It just took a little longer for it to fall apart. And I didn't even try to hold on when it did. I watched them go, one by one. I didn't argue. I assumed it was inevitable. That it was because of what was happening to me, because of my back. But was it? Was it ever?

"Neff," I say. "Hold on."

I didn't ask them to stay back then—but I'm asking now. Maybe it's pathetic. Maybe I should be embarrassed, but I'm not. Look what that got me last time.

If he keeps walking now, I'm pretty sure that's it. We're done for good. But at least it won't be because I didn't try.

He doesn't stop, but he slows down. He turns halfway around.

"Your hydroturbine looks really good," I say.

He gives me a look like: *Seriously? This is what you want to talk about?*

Then I hit him with the punch line: "I think it's going to make some waves."

He laughs, just a little. Then he shakes his head and says, "You are such a dork."

I hustle to catch up to him, but I don't really need to. He's waiting for me now.

We talk about the contest and school and just regular stuff until he has to turn off to head home. It's cold out, but I'm smiling the whole way. It just feels good to talk to Neff again.

IT'S OFFICIAL

IT'S A LITTLE TRICKY wheeling the bike frame into school on Wednesday morning, and it looks small and kind of junky in the sunlight. I can't wait any longer, though. The ad comes out today, and I still have to fix up the frame, reattach the engine, take it for a test drive . . . I'm already worried I haven't left myself enough time.

"Just get back from the dump, Freak?" someone says as I push the bike through the crosswalk.

I'm bent down low, pushing it by its seat and one handlebar. Haley and Becca see me coming and set up on either side. I push faster but can't get away.

"Is that a toy?" says Haley from one side.

"It's so junky," says Becca from the other. I'm caught in the crossfire. "Where are the pedals?"

"And the training wheels!" whoops Haley.

I ignore them, but they keep going.

"Is that what Santa brought you?" says Haley. "Must have been the best Christmas ever at your house."

"Shut up," I say. Christmas is a sensitive subject.

"What did you say to me?" she says.

"Better *back* off, Hay," says Becca. "He's got some great come*backs*."

"Stop that," I say.

"Stop what?" she says.

When we reach the sidewalk they cut in front and hog the little ramp so I have to bump the bike up onto the curb. The little jolt runs through me and I feel a familiar burst of pain in my back. It's already hurting from bending over so long.

"Later, loser," says Haley, and at least it feels good when they leave.

I wheel the bike up the wheelchair ramp, and Mrs. Gallego is waiting at the top. "You can't bring that into the school," she says, her face peering down at the bike from inside the hood of her big white coat.

"It's for Mr. Feig," I say. Which would be news to him. "It's a science project."

"Oh!" says Mrs. Gallego. "Is it for the contest?"

"Uh, yeah?"

She considers it. "All right," she says, stepping back to keep her long, spotless coat away from the disreputable bike. "But don't drip oil on the tiles."

"Don't worry," I say, carving a big semicircle around her. "No engine."

The heat is cranking inside and I start sweating immediately. The hallway is as chaotic as always, but a funny thing happens when you push machinery through a crowd. They get out of the way. I make it to Mr. Feig's room in decent time.

I can finally straighten up a little. My hair is sweat-plastered to my forehead, and my back is throbbing. "Can I keep this here for the day?" I say, sounding at least as miserable as I feel.

Mr. Feig gets up from his desk and comes over. "So this is the bike, huh?"

"Yup," I say.

He frowns. "You're gonna make it a little more . . . presentable, right?"

"Totally," I say. "I've got paint and stuff. Just need to make sure it runs first."

"You can keep it in the closet till after school," he says.

"Thanks," I say, already wheeling it over.

I barely have time to grab my stuff and get to homeroom. I don't even get a chance to splash some cold water on my face. It definitely feels good to sit down, though.

I see Nephi in the hallway and ask him what he's up to.

"Making waves," he says, and I laugh.

"Now who's a dork?" I say, even though it's pretty clear we both are.

All morning I'm thinking about the paper. It comes out on Wednesdays. I picture all the papers stacked by the counter at the pharmacy and tossed onto people's lawns, the website probably already updated. I haven't seen my ad yet, though. They usually have the paper in the library, or I could check online there, but that's in the upper building. I figure I'll have to wait until we head up for lunch, at least. I really *really* hope they printed the part about not calling after five.

But then I see the paper lying on Mrs. Gallego's desk in social studies. Her long white coat is gone, but now she has a long white sweater on over light blue pants. When it's cold out, she basically dresses like a character from *Frozen*. She has told us more than once that she is a big believer in "dressing for the season." Once spring comes, I'm expecting her to look like an explosion in a flower shop. I ask her if I can see the paper.

"You're full of unusual requests today," says Queen Elsa.

"I guess," I say. "Please?"

She grabs the paper and holds it out to me. *Let it go*, I think and she does. I take it and flip to the back but there's a problem. "There are no classifieds!" I say, my voice breaking.

"Oh, I always throw those out," she says.

I look over at the plastic recycling basket next to her desk and see a few pages of black-and-white newsprint sticking out. I reach down to pick them out.

"Beep! Beep!" I hear, along with some laughter. I don't even care right now. My fingers peel the pages open. The "For Sale" section is right at the front, and my ad is right near the top. I feel a sudden wave of affection for the old lady on the phone.

My eyes fly over the ad. (Not literally, that would be gross.) Good, it says exactly what I told them.

I drop the pages back in the basket and turn around. "Beep! Beep!" says Haley, right in my face. "Garbage boy!"

"That's enough," says Mrs. Gallego.

For a second, Haley and I are just standing there face-to-face. Her nose is basically fine now, just a faint purple line across the bridge. But the happy little bounce in her step as she heads back to her desk lets me know. Her nose was never the problem.

PAINT IT BLACK (AND RED)

I WHEEL THE BIKE all the way up the hill after school, leaning forward with my head down and elementary schoolers rocketing by on both sides. And after all that, I get the stink-eye from the teacher at the door, and the one in the hall too, but I've got my lines down now. "Maker space," I mumble. "Contest this weekend!"

And please note: I did not say I was *in* the contest. I just said there was one. And the truth is: I wish I was. It wasn't on my radar at all before, but if I wasn't rebuilding this bike now, I'd love to be building a model. I'd like to be one of those kids trying to get an idea out of their head and onto the table.

I know what I'd build too: a model of a place where people could get help for things they needed without getting judged or feeling bad about it. Like if they needed to get online without having to spend half an hour pretending to read a magazine, or if they needed a shower, or a lead on a job that wasn't half-time.

Or if they needed to take a class to get the skills for that job or they needed to know their rights as renters! That would make Norton better for a lot of people.

Or maybe I'd build something cool and mechanical with an engine. I don't know, but I like the idea of building a better Norton. Pretty much every happy moment of my life has happened here. The lake, epic Halloween hauls, eating pizza with Dad . . . But this place could *definitely* be better. Living on the edge of the edge of town, the half-time factory, the empty stores, the stupid Stubbs brothers . . . Every unhappy moment of my life has happened here too. And let's be honest, that's most of them lately.

But when I get the bike into the maker space, there's Esme and Nephi, already working away. As happy as I am to see them, watching them build and experiment reminds me that we're here for different reasons. They're here to dream up something new and cool. I'm here on the wildest chance I can save the messed-up life I already have. Fingers crossed.

But as I'm thinking that, Esme and Nephi are already putting down their tools and pushing back their chairs. The two of them head toward me, and I push the frame out in front of me so they can get a better look.

"How old is it?" says Nephi, eyeing the worn-out paint.

"Like nine years," says Esme.

From what I've learned about this bike online, she's exactly right. "Good guess," I say.

Nephi gives the bike one last appraising look. "Pretty cool," he says, and I smile.

Esme doesn't say anything else, just stands there staring at a nine-year-old bike frame. She's been a lot friendlier in here, and I think she's pretty cool. But she definitely gets weird about this bike. My new theory: Maybe she's really into minibikes—like she knows the models and years and everything—and she's jealous of mine. I mean, it is a Road Rokkit.

Whatever her deal is, I don't have a ton of time to think about it. I have to paint the bike, and before I do that, I have to clean it. It's not too bad. I already splooshed a bucket of soapy water over it when I took it out of the shed this morning. Then I absolutely ruined an old T-shirt (I'm out of old towels) rubbing it down. It was literally freezing out. By the time I was finished, my hands were numb and the white T-shirt was brown. It was frozen into a U-shape when I dumped it in the garbage can.

But any dirt is too much to paint over, so now I've got the bottle of spray cleaner from the cabinet and my trusty washcloth. Pretty soon, that's brown again too, but at least the bike is clean.

"Good enough," I mutter to myself. Next I need to remove some of the old flaky paint. "Uh, Mr. Feig?" I say.

He looks up and honestly seems a little annoyed by the interruption. I don't know what kind of state test he's preparing for—or preparing to prepare us for, I guess—but it must be intense. I get to the point. "Do we have any paint thinner in here?"

"Are you kidding me right now, Ked?" he says.

Yeah, I guess that would be a little toxic for middle school.

"Can I use some of this sandpaper? It's right next to the toolkit."

"I know where it is, Ked. I put it there. It's a pretty course grain, more for wood."

"Please?" I say. "It's my only hope."

I don't recognize the mangled *Star Wars* line until it's already out. Nephi snarfs out a laugh.

"Sure," says Mr. Feig. He sounds resigned, too tired to argue. "Just don't make a mess."

"I won't," I say, taking an old section of newspaper out of my backpack. It's last week's "Help Wanted" section. I'm destroying the evidence. I unfold the pages on the floor and wheel the bike over it. I'm fine just painting over the parts where the frame still has paint. And I'm fine painting over the parts where it doesn't. It's the in-between parts, where the paint is flaking and chipping away, that I need to smooth out.

I do my best, but it doesn't go like I planned it in my head. I'm trying to smooth out the edges of the paint, but mostly I'm just peeling off more flakes. Maybe if I spray the paint on thick enough, it will all even out?

I blow off the sandpaper dust from the spot I've been working on and reach into my bag for the spray paint. I pick up the can and shake it a few times. Something metal rattles around inside.

"Absolutely not!" I hear. It's Mr. Feig. He's standing above me— like way above me, since he's basically a giraffe and I'm sitting on the floor. Suddenly he's very much willing to argue.

"I have to!" I say with my usual gift for persuasion.

"Take it out to the parking lot," he says. "And not near any of the cars, either."

"Not near his anyway," says Nephi.

Esme chuckles softly.

I get up and get my jacket and spend close to an hour working outside again. I hunker down in an empty parking spot. And maybe I'm *kind of* near a car on one side but (a) no one likes our vice principal and (b) I need some shelter from the wind or the paint's going to go everywhere.

I can't just blast away. I have to spray carefully to make sure I don't get the wrong color in the wrong place. I use a plastic shopping bag to cover up behind where I'm spraying. By the time I'm finished, the bag is speckled with red and black paint, and the fingers of my blue gloves are too. Now I look like a mechanic. Cool.

Anyway, I do the best I can. I spray until my head is reeling from the fumes, and then I spray a little bit more. Then I stand up and step back. It's . . . okay. Maybe a little uneven and still dripping as it dries. I look down and see some incriminating red splotches on the pavement.

I lean against the car to stay out of the wind and hold the bike up by the handlebars to give the paint time to dry. By the time I get back inside, it's already time to go. I was really hoping to get more done today. I'm also freezing.

"Can I warm up a little first?" I say, and at least it gives the rest of the late shift a few more minutes to work.

27

GETTING THE MESSAGE

MR. FEIG LETS ME leave the frame in the back corner of the room, which is pretty cool of him since fifteen minutes ago it was still dripping red paint. It will dry better inside, and I definitely don't feel like wheeling it all the way home anyway.

Esme bolts out of there like a racehorse, as usual. But Nephi waits up again. I figure we'll have even more time to talk today, but then I remember something important. Our phone number is in that ad for the whole town to see. I could have a message already—and sometimes Dad gets home early.

"Sorry, man," I say. "Kind of in a hurry."

"No problem," he says. "See you tomorrow."

Those are three of the best words I've heard in a long time, so even though I bust out in an awkward jog-walk, I do it with a smile. Fifteen minutes later, I'm standing in the living room with the phone to my ear. I hear these words, clear as a summer day:

"You have one new message."

I hold my breath and press 1, and by the time I breathe again, I've got a potential buyer. It's some old dude who's not only interested but "very interested." With my free hand, I do a fist pump like I just threw a touchdown pass in the Super Bowl.

I write the number down and call him back right away, before I chicken out. His name is Gene and he has wanted a Road Rokkit "since they first started making 'em," which was like last century. I'm not sure a guy that old should be rocketing around on a motorbike the size of a prize-winning pumpkin, but that's not my problem.

I'll admit I'm pretty nervous talking to him, and he's like, "How old are you, anyway?" But he still wants the bike.

"So six hundred," I venture, but he swats that down.

"We'll talk price when I see the bike," he says.

That's smart for him, but all I can picture is that stupid dripping paint.

"How about Royston's parking lot on Saturday?" I say.

"Friday," he says. "I'm out of town this weekend."

Man, I think, *that's not much time.* But he's the one with the money. "All right," I say. "How's five?"

So it's all set by the time Dad gets home. He's in a horrible mood again. It's still so cold out. The ice is a day thicker and St. Paddy's is a day closer. Not that he admits that's what's bothering him. There's just a dark cloud hanging over him all night. He spends most of it staring silently at the TV, and the most noise he makes is when he lifts his arm to click the remote.

I'm already stressed out enough about agreeing to Friday. That means I'll definitely have to test-drive it tomorrow—and the engine isn't even attached yet! I don't need any more stress so I head to my room. I feel like a prisoner in there once I close the door. It's times like these I really miss the internet. Instead, I fall asleep reading.

When I wake up, it's Thursday, March 16, the day before dad's bet, the day before I meet Gene. The good thing about falling asleep early is that at least I've got some energy. I am definitely going to need it.

You ever have days when you just can't concentrate on schoolwork? (You ever have days when you can? Ha-ha!) I've got to get the engine reattached and then see if the whole thing works. That's a lot to do in one day. And even if the engine starts, it could always blow off one of my feet or something on the test drive.

Anyway, schoolwork isn't the only thing I'm not concentrating on. On my way to study hall to look for videos on reconnecting engines, I nearly run right into Landrover. Or maybe he runs into me. That seems more likely, now that I say it.

"Hey, Freak. Saw your junk heap in the corner."

I look away. I see a teacher at the end of the hall, so I'm hoping this will just be a verbal takedown.

"I told you to stay out of maker space."

Now I look at him. I guess he knows about the late shift now. He reads my thoughts. "Yeah, I asked around," he says. "I know about your sad little weirdo crew."

That makes me mad. Mad for Nephi, who's not weird anyway, just smart. Mad for Esme, who got chased out of regular maker space just like me. "What do you care?" I say. "You aren't even there!"

"SO?" he says. *Sick burn, bro,* I think, but he's not done talking. "You really think you're gonna get that thing going? Aren't you gonna need—oh, I don't know, a *working engine,* maybe?"

I should just shut up and let him get it out of his system, but I'm angry now. And maybe I'm a little sick of always rolling over and playing dead for this jumbo-sized jerk. "I've got a working engine!" I say, looking him right in the eyes and hoping it's true.

"Yeah, right," he says, but I can see he's not sure.

I try to calm down for this next part so I can sound casual, confident. "Taking it for a test-drive today. Just to work out a few bugs."

"Good luck with that," he says, shaking his head. "Your funeral."

He raises both fists and I flinch, but he just spreads his fingers apart and makes a soft explosion sound with his mouth: *"Boom."* And then he's gone.

28

RECONNECTING

I HIT THE GROUND working when I get to maker space. I'm a man on a mission! (Plus, I just watched the video, and I don't want the info to leak out of my brain.) Reattaching the engine is nuts—well, nuts and bolts. And some screws. What I'm saying is, there's a whole lot of tightening going on. Road Rokkits were designed to be easy to take apart and put back together. "Modular" is the word everyone uses online. But it's still a machine as big as a labradoodle, so there's plenty of work to do. I've got the bike on the floor, leaning against a leg of the table.

I reconnect the engine without too much trouble and take extra care reconnecting the throttle cable to it. Then I get started reconnecting the chain. It takes a lot more muscle than it looked like on the video, and I grunt my way through it.

"I think there's something under the table," says Nephi.

"Sounds like some kind of animal," says Esme. "Maybe a bear?"

"Based on the smell, I am going to say skunk."

Even Mr. Feig laughs at that one.

I clean the grease off my hands with the towel and stand back up. Neff and Esme both duck and cover like I'm going to spray them. "You're lucky I'm not a skunk," I say.

"Not technically," says Esme.

They high-five. I like the joking, even if it's about me. It takes my mind off the pressure. There's just one last thing to do. I take the spark plug out of my pocket, screw it into its place of honor at the top of the engine, and reconnect the wire.

"You can't start that inside the building," says Mr. Feig in his serious teacher voice. "Take it out to the parking lot—and please be careful."

That was my plan anyway. He just doesn't need to know about the test-drive I'm planning after that. I put my jacket and backpack on and begin wheeling the bike toward the door. It's heavier and rolls differently with the engine in and the drive train reconnected. It feels more legit, more mechanical.

"Break a leg," says Esme.

"Don't blow up," says Nephi.

"Remember, you signed the release form," adds Mr. Feig.

"It feels great to have so much support, guys," I respond.

I roll the bike out into the back parking lot. Most of the cars are gone now, but I find an empty space between two of the ones that are left. It gives me a little shelter from the wind and anyone watching. I lean the bike gently against one of the cars and take my backpack off. The first thing I take out is a green plastic Mountain Dew bottle. It's full of gasoline that I took from the can in the lawn mower shed and mixed with some of the two-stroke engine oil I got at the store. The oil is supposed to burn off when the gas does. It's a minibike thing.

The precise ratio of gas to oil is just one of the things I could have gotten disastrously wrong. (Serious question: Have I said "Don't try this at home" yet?)

Very carefully, I fill the tank. I recap the bottle and put it back in my pack. I check the switches and say a quick prayer. I haven't been to church in a while, but I'm hoping I have some credit left in my account. Then I stand the bike up and grab the handle of the pull cord. It's just like starting a lawn mower.

I exhale, inhale—*Here goes absolutely everything.* With my knee on the seat and my left hand on the throttle, I tug hard on the cord handle with my right.

The engine chokes to life like an old man with a cold: *sputter, sputter, cough.* But then, disaster: The old man dies.

The engine is quiet. The cold wind whips over the tops of the cars. A hot panic kicks up inside me. But then I remember our old lawn mower, how sometimes it takes two or four or twelve good tugs to get it started.

I lean down a little farther and adjust my grip on the handle. I try to clear my mind, like a Jedi. "Stretch out with your feelings," I whisper. It's another *Star Wars* line and obviously super corny, but it's not like anyone can hear me.

I tug back hard, practically punching myself in the stomach.

Sputter, sputter, cough, sputter, sputter.

Better! I catch a quick whiff of fuel.

I pull again: *Sputter, sputter, VROOOM!* I rev the throttle: *VROOM-VROOM!*

I just about faint with relief. And then I hear it. The sound is close and unmistakable, even over the raspy purr of the rebuilt engine.

Applause.

I turn and see Nephi and Esme, standing by the bumper of one of the cars and clapping for me.

I smile, the kind of real, full smile that I wasn't even sure my face remembered how to make. "Thanks," I say.

"Stretch out with your feelings," says Nephi.

I'm embarrassed that they heard that, but I've got bigger things to think about. I pull on my paint-speckled gloves and reach into my backpack for my old bike helmet.

"You know, when I said 'break a leg' before, I was just joking," says Esme. "It's an expression."

"Yeah," I say, adjusting my helmet and fastening the strap. The engine starting is a big relief, but there's more to a minibike than that. There's steering and stopping and not blowing up. "But I have to know if this thing works."

I grip the handlebars and sort of hunker down into the right position—at least what I thought was the right position.

"Hold on," says Esme. "You're sitting too far back."

"I am?"

"Yeah, it's a small bike. You'll fall right off the back—or pop your last wheelie."

I kind of scoot forward a little. "Like this?"

"Here," she says, stepping forward. She puts one hand on the handlebars and the other on my lower back. I don't like anyone touching my back, but . . . maybe I don't mind this so much. She shoves me forward on the seat.

"Oof!" I say. I'm sitting up a little straighter, which, now that I think about it, makes sense.

"Stay there," she says. "Or this is gonna be a real short trip."

It's another line from *Star Wars*. Han Solo. I look up at her: brown eyes, purple hair, wise in the ways of The Force. I, uh, may be in love?

"You going to the nature trail?" says Nephi, and I snap out of it.

I nod. It's a footpath through the woods behind the school, a big wandering loop through the trees. Every student here has made that walk a dozen times: looking where the teacher points, writing down the names of the birds or trees or whatever else they plan to test us on later. This feels like a test too. A big one.

REV IT UP, KED!

THEY SAY YOU NEVER forget how to ride a bike, but when you shrink that bike down to something that basically fits between your knees and slap a powerful engine on it, those old lessons definitely get a little fuzzy. I'm perched on top of the thing now, leaning forward over the handlebars and holding on like grim death. I wobble slowly across the parking lot, giving it the absolute minimum amount of gas to keep it upright. It feels like a piece of gravel would be enough to tip me over.

I thought the rest of the late shift had gone inside already, but I catch a glimpse of them now. They're peeking out of the half-open door to see if I totally eat it. I guess maybe I'm showing off a little, because I rev the engine, just a quick half turn on the throttle. The bike scoots forward under me. I have to squeeze hard to stay on, but a funny thing happens after that.

It gets easier.

It's actually easier to balance going faster. It really is like those first wobbly moments without the training wheels. I keep light pressure on the throttle and bounce over the edge of the parking lot and onto the patchy grass and snow of the field that leads to the path. I'm moving now, steering. The little wheels are rolling like mighty donuts eating up the squishy ground. Even when I hit a patch of snow, they cut right through.

I'm doing it! The bike works! I feel a rush of exhilaration as the bike bounces onto the start of the path. The trail is wide and bumpy. I hit a fat stick early on and almost crash. There are trees zooming by on both sides now. If I hit one of those, I'm not sure this old bicycle helmet is going to do much good.

As I bounce and bumble over bumps and dips in the dirt, I am super aware of every nut and bolt and screw I just put back in the Road Rokkit. I seriously hope I tightened them enough.

And then I see something up ahead. A flash of bright blue and red. Man-made colors—there's someone else out here. I slow down for a better look as I pass. As bouncy and blurry as the whole world seems at the moment, I see one image clearly.

It's Landrover.

He's sitting on top of a small, shiny four-wheeler.

As soon as I pass, I hear it roar to life as he revs the engine and peels out onto the path behind me. I let out a groan, but it's swallowed by the wind and the sounds of our engines. Why couldn't I just shut up when he cornered me in the hallway? Why'd I have to open my stupid mouth and tell him I was taking the bike for a test-drive?

I grip the throttle and twist down hard. The little reconstructed engine roars to life. The bike scoots forward.

The chase is on.

It feels really scary to be going so fast so low to the ground, like I'm hanging out a car door or something. My elbows are out wide for balance, but it's a twisty, bumpy path. A sharp turn comes up fast. I don't think I'm going to make it, but I lean into the corner and carve my way through. The little wheels bite into the dirt and spit up pebbles and twigs behind me. It would be super cool if it weren't so terrifying.

The path straightens out, and I gun the throttle. I risk a quick look back. Landrover's bright blue four-wheeler tears through the turn easily. His four wheels are giving him twice the stability.

When I turn my head back around, I'm already zooming straight into the next turn. It's too late to make it. A big, fat evergreen at the edge of the trail is looming up in front of me. This is gonna hurt.

I can't make the turn, but I throw my weight to the side and jerk the handlebars hard, hoping to at least miss the tree. My sleeve brushes the rough bark, and I just barely slip by, avoiding a head-on crash. I am flying off the trail and into the woods, already falling as I go. Falling and flying, flying and falling . . . I tilt toward the dirt. For a second, the wheels are off the ground, spinning uselessly in the air.

Then, impact.

OOOOOOOOOF!

My left knee hits the ground first, and the pain shoots through me in a hot, electric burst. My body hits next, and the pain fills my upper back like water flowing into a hollow place.

The left handlebar hits hard, digging in as it slides through the dirt. My body, the tires, the bike: We all slide along the dirt and mud and dead leaves. Another tree looms up in front of me. I close my eyes and brace myself, but by the time I hit it I'm almost stopped anyway. The front tire bounces off it and the bike comes to a halt with a sad little *poomp!*

I lie there, stunned. My side is all scraped up under my clothes. My knee is throbbing. My back is alive with a jangly, tingling pain. And the rear wheel of the bike is spinning and spinning. I'm just trying to breathe right, just waiting for the pain to fade, when I hear a motor rev somewhere behind me. That's when I remember: Landrover.

I whip my head around as much as I'm able to. It's just enough to see him there, still sitting on his new blue four-wheeler. He's on the path, peering through the trees at me. Is he going to come in here after me? He waits until he sees my eyes, then revs the throttle. Something inside the four-wheeler must catch wrong, because the rev is a strangled groan. A puff of dark smoke shoots out of the exhaust as Landrover tears off down the trail without even looking back.

I'm left on my own, on my side, on the ground. And as nice as it would be to have some help right now, I'm glad I'm alone. I'm glad because that's when I start to cry. It's the kind of crying where the only way out is through, where I just have to let it run its course and get it out of my system.

Afterward, I try to wipe my face with my sleeve, but my face is too salty and snotty for that. I dig out an old paper towel from a crumpled-up lunch bag at the bottom of my pack, and that works better. I slide out from under the bike and try to stand up. My knee is banged up, my jeans are torn even more, and my whole left side feels stiff and raw.

I stand up slowly and look down at the bike. I am so full of fear as I reach down and lift it up onto its wheels. I check the key. I check the switches. I check the choke, which is covered in dirt and in the wrong position. I flip it.

I put my knee on the seat and my hand on the throttle.

I consider another quick prayer, but it's not like the first one worked out so great. Instead, I just reach down, grab the starter handle, and give the cord as good a tug as my battered body can manage.

The only sound is the *roummp* of the starter cord being pulled.

I try a few more times.

On the third or fourth, I get a sputter and a little puff of black smoke from the exhaust, but that's it. I give it a few more hard tugs, but there are no more signs of life, just the *roummp roummp* of the starter.

I brush myself off a little and begin walking the bike back to the school. I'm a total mess and just barely holding it together, so once I'm inside I do everything I can to get out of there fast. I tell

Mr. Feig that I tripped and fell and watch him size up the mud and dirt along my left side and reconsider every nice thing he's ever tried to do for a student. I gather up my stuff quick and head out. I tell Esme I'm fine, and I tell Nephi I appreciate it but I can get home on my own.

They're not idiots, though. They don't buy it for a second.

LIKE FRIENDS DO

THE BIG DOUBLE DOORS are closing behind me and the cold air is hitting me in the face and I'm thinking: *Okay, great, now I can at least start crying again if I have to.* It just seems so hopeless, you now? I'm supposed to sell this thing tomorrow—I *need* to sell this thing tomorrow—and now I went and broke it. I don't know if I have time to fix it—I don't even know what's wrong with it! And it was working too, and then Landrover. So it doesn't just seem hopeless, it seems unfair too, and here come the tears.

But no! Because the double doors punch back open— Ba-Doom!—and here come Nephi and Esme. I can't believe they followed me again, and at first I don't even appreciate it. "Leave me alone!" I say, my voice breaking halfway through.

"Come on, man," says Nephi. "What's wrong? What happened?"

I stop pushing the bike. They're faster than me anyway. I look back at them and I see Mr. Feig's huge glasses peering out of one half-open door. Nephi waves him away: *We've got this. Kids only.* Mr. Feig gets the message and disappears.

"I crashed," I say. I wait a little, just to make sure Feig's gone and add: "I had some help."

And now Esme is right next to me. She takes hold of the bike by the handlebars and holds it up so I don't have to. My hands are free now. I run my jacket sleeve under my nose and suck in some snot.

"Seriously, Ked, what happened?" says Nephi.

I can see the concern on both of their faces. They are looking at me like friends do when you're hurting, and I guess that's why I tell them. I tell them about the test-drive and Landrover and the crash. "I told him I was doing it! I bragged to him!" I say at the end.

"This is not your fault," says Nephi. "This is all on him. He's a scumbag."

"Big bag of scum," agrees Esme. "Like a Hefty bag."

I laugh, just like one hiccup's worth, but it makes me feel better.

"It's no big deal," says Nephi. "We can help you fix it. Next week, after the contest, we'll have all the time in the world."

I shake my head. "I need it by tomorrow."

They look at each other and ask at the same time: "Why?"

And listen, I wasn't going to tell them this. It wasn't going to tell anyone this—except Dad, because he'd need to know where I got the money. But the truth is, when your eyes are red and puffy from crying and you've got crusty snot on your chin, there's only so much lower you can go. "I was fixing it up to sell it," I say. And then, because Nephi's dad is in the same boat, and Esme is standing there in her hand-me-down coat holding up my bike, I add: "We're behind on the rent."

Nephi blows out some air. Esme just nods. I don't feel bad that I told them.

"When are you supposed to sell it?" says Esme.

"Tomorrow at five. Royston's parking lot."

"Well, that's no problem," says Nephi. It's the last thing I expected anyone to say in the face of this huge and obvious problem. But then Esme agrees.

"Yeah," she says. "We'll help you tomorrow."

"But . . . what about your models? The contest?"

"Dude," says Nephi. "We're both basically done. How close do you think we were going to cut it?"

"Really?" I say.

"Really," says Esme. "I was cutting out a tiny *weathervane* when you came in. No one needs to see a tiny weathervane."

There's a pause.

"I, uh, I would kind of like to see that," I say.

"Me too," says Nephi.

Esme rolls her eyes. "The point is. We have time."

This time, I don't argue.

"Okay," she says. "Let me see you start the bike."

"It won't start," I say.

"Let me see you try."

So I do. Esme and Nephi are both watching closely, so I make sure my hands are in the right place and I give the starter cord some good hard tugs. A few pulls in, I get a single sputter and that same little puff of black smoke, but that's it. There's nothing after that.

"Dead," I say.

Esme is nodding again. Does she knows something—or is she just agreeing that it's dead?

"Tomorrow," she says, and honestly what do I have to lose—except everything. At least it will be nice to spend the last late shift before the contest with these two.

"Okay," I say. "Thanks." I take the bike from Esme and begin walking it toward the slope.

"You're limping," she says.

I guess I am, a little.

"If you hold on like ten minutes, I'll help you get that home," says Nephi. "Just need to finish something up and grab my coat."

I appreciate it, but I really don't feel like waiting ten minutes right now.

"I'll do it," says Esme. "Already got my coat. Could you put my stuff away?"

"Sure, no problem," says Nephi.

"You don't need to—" I begin, but Esme isn't having it.

"Nope, you're outvoted, two to one. Now, which way?"

I point down the hill.

"Good," she says as she takes the bike again and starts pushing.

I walk alongside, or limp, I guess, but just a little.

It's not that long a walk, and neither of us says very much. It's a little harder without Neff. He's the one we both know. And anyway, I've got a lot to think about. What happened in that crash? What if I need more parts? Esme seems to be thinking about something too.

"This is it," I say, taking the handlebars back from her in front of the house.

She looks at the place.

"We're on the second floor," I say. "For now."

She looks up there. "Now we're even," she says.

"What?" I say.

"I've seen your home and you've seen mine."

I'm seriously confused. "I haven't seen your home," I say.

"Sure you have," she says, already walking away. "That used to be my bike."

All I can do is stand there holding the bike and watching her walk away. The pieces click into place one by one, like a combination lock.

I wondered what the deal was with her and this bike, and now I guess I know.

I remember the mountain man at the door of that old slanting house saying, "Who has time? Two kids in high school and one in eighth."

I remember the curtains moving in the window above me.

That was her. That was her dad. Her house.

And once upon a time, it was her bike.

Now her dad sold it to me, and I'm thinking he didn't ask.

I know what that's like, your past sold out from under you. My old house, her old bike: happy memories and better times, just gone. I want to tell her that, but she's gone too.

31

IT'S A START

I WAKE UP SORE. My back aches. I take two ibuprofen from the jar by my bed. The side of my left leg is all scraped up and already starting to scab over. I wear my loosest cargo pants just because it hurts less to pull them on. I wear my green Yoda T-shirt under my baggy button-up. It's St. Patrick's Day after all, and for the record, it's still cold out.

I pass Landrover in the hall midmorning, and he's smirking and trying to catch my eye. Normally that would scare me, but I'm too mad right now. "Jerk," I say.

He thinks that's funny. "That's it?" he says.

But what else is there? What am I going to do, punch him? He's twice my size and four times my strength. And I'm not going to tell on him. I mean, I thought about it, but I was the one using school property as a test track. And technically he never actually touched me. So, yeah: jerk. That's what I got.

The day passes like a blur and pretty soon I'm pushing the

bike back up the hill to maker space. I pass a few teachers in the hallway once I get back to the upper building, but they don't say anything. They're used to me wheeling this thing to the library now. The door is half-open, and as I push inside I hear a soft humming. Esme and Mr. Feig are standing around Nephi. He's got his tank filled with water, and the hum is the motor. It's running.

I lean the bike against the door and head over. The others step aside and make space for me. The little motor is at one end, sending small waves down the length of the tank. That's supposed to be the river flowing through town. At the other end, the waves are turning a little propeller connected to a box. A wire runs from there to a gauge on the top that shows how much electricity the little turbine is generating.

It's amazing. Nephi knows it. He's looking down at the tank, fiddling with something on the back of the engine and trying so hard not to smile. He's totally going to win. "It's awesome," I say.

"Okay, sure," says Esme. "But check this out."

Nephi flips a switch and the engine goes silent. We move down the table toward Esme's model.

"It's beautiful," says Mr. Feig, and he's right.

The town is a huddle of miniature black buildings. The angles and edges are clean and precise. All those cuts with the X-Acto knife and I don't see a single slip. It looks like a model for a movie set—a horror movie, but still. "Check this out," she says.

She turns the model slightly so we have a good view of the street cutting through the center of her gothic downtown. Right in the middle of that is a little display. The soft gray stands out against all the black. It's the solar-powered bank clock, right on time.

It's perfect, and now I'm thinking that maybe she's going to win.

"It's okay," I say, acting unimpressed. "But it could use a tiny weathervane."

She and Nephi both laugh, but Mr. Feig doesn't get it. "Seriously awesome work, you two," he says before drifting back to his pile of papers.

"All right," says Esme, turning toward me. "Show-and-tell is over."

Nephi turns to me too. "Let's get to work."

I take a deep breath. I've been waiting for this. "Here goes everything," I say as we head over to the bike. It's the three of us now, the late shift. Up to this point, we've been doing our own thing. But now we're working together, and it makes me feel good. It's that same feeling that was snatched away from me before, that feeling of being included.

It's also just—I don't know—hope, I guess. Fixing this bike in the next few hours may be impossible, but it feels like if anyone can help me do it, it's these two. I remind myself of everything I've done so far. I rebuilt the entire engine. I reconnected everything and got it running again. This isn't great, but I've overcome a lot more. Being in here and doing so much—with my own hands and borrowed tools and a small army of how-to videos—it's given me a lot of confidence. I'm a maker now.

That said, we are definitely up against it.

"Guys, I don't even know where to start," I admit.

"I think I might," says Esme.

I look at her. We haven't had a chance to talk about what she told me yet. Maybe this is the time?

She looks back at me, reading my thoughts—or my expression any way, my half-open mouth. She shakes her head. *Not now.* "I think it's the carb," she says, all business. "It wasn't turning over at all, and there was that black smoke the one time it tried."

"Can we just take that off and work on it?" says Nephi.

"Yeah," I say. It seems a lot more manageable than another full teardown.

So that's where we start. Neff holds the bike steady as I get to work, and Esme is holding out the tools I need before I even ask for them. I already drained the fuel line at home because I knew things were going to have to come apart again.

We take the carb over to the table. "Should you do it?" I say to Esme.

"No, I've only seen my dad do this. And anyway, you just did it."

Okay, I think. *Time for more open-heart surgery.*

I open it up, slowly and carefully and get to work.

"I think I see the problem," I say after a few minutes, my heart sinking down to my shoes.

"Oh yeah?" says Nephi, peering over my shoulder.

"Yeah," I say. It was that stupid improvised gasket. I was worried about tearing it when I took it out again, but looking down at it now, it's already torn. I pinch it between my fingers and pull it free. "It must have slipped out of place during the chase, or the crash. It didn't fit that great to begin with."

"Just replace it," says Nephi.

"I can't," I say. "I don't have any more. This was all the store had."

"What about online?"

"No time," I say.

"Oh yeah."

Esme knows a lot more about this than Nephi does, but this whole time she's been strangely quiet. "Well," she says, finally speaking up. "I suppose you could use these."

She tosses something down on the table beside me. It lands with a soft flop and I look over. It's a small, flat baggie with a paper label inside facing out. I pick it up and feel some small, light objects shifting around inside. I read the label, but I can barely believe it.

"Road Rokkit Rebuild Kit" it says at the top. In smaller print below there is a list of all the parts inside. "Oh my God," I breathe. The actual parts I need are in here, the actual gaskets, not cut-to-fit imitations.

"You've had this the whole time?" I say. "And you just . . . watched me struggle?"

She shrugs, and I can see she's trying not to smile. "Yeah, I saw you cutting those do-it-yourself gaskets with my knife. I didn't know what you needed this for. I thought you just took my bike."

"Your bike?" says Nephi, but we both give him a look like: *We'll tell you later.*

"I kept this kit because *I* was thinking of fixing the bike

176

sometime," she says. "And anyway, remember yesterday when I told you we were even?"

"Yeah?"

"Well *now* we're even," she says, finally letting that smile break free.

I just stare at her. "You are, like, really complicated," I say finally.

"You have no idea," she says. "Now get to work."

So I replace the gasket and put the carburetor back together. I tear the metering diaphragm on the way out, and I don't even care. I have the perfect replacement right at my fingertips.

"I think it's good," I say once the carb's back in one piece.

Nephi wheels the bike over so. "Let's hope that was the only problem," he says.

I was just thinking the same thing.

Once the carburetor is reattached and everything is back where it should be, there's only one thing left to do. At least I hope there's only one thing. "I guess this is it," I say as we jacket up and begin wheeling the bike out to the parking lot.

"I think I have to see this," says Mr. Feig, pushing back his chair.

So now we're all out in the parking lot. I put some fresh fuel in the tank and put the cap back on the Mountain Dew bottle.

"Anyone else want to try?" I say.

"This is all you," says Esme.

I check to make sure everything is in the right position: the switches, the choke.

I check again.

"Stop stalling," says Nephi.

"Okay okay," I say.

I take a deep breath, put my hand on the throttle, and give the cord a tug for the ages.

Sputter, sputter, vroom!

I crank the throttle: *VROOM! VROOM!*

One hand still on the throttle, I hold the other one up. High fives all around. Even Mr. Feig gets in on it, though I guess it's more of a low five for him.

"Thanks, guys," I say. I try to think of something bigger than that, but I'm too overwhelmed. "Thanks—oh, and good luck at the contest Sunday!"

CRACKED UP TO BE

SO I'M FEELING PRETTY good and walking the bike home to give it one last soap-and-water cleanup. I briefly consider riding it, but I didn't bring my helmet, and I'm not sure I can take any more excitement at the moment anyway. I've got plenty of time before the meeting, so I start looking at the bike, sizing it up the way I think Gene will.

I've got to be honest. The paint job isn't great. A little streaky, a little uneven . . . It's not that bad, though. The parts where the paint was peeling were mostly the black parts, and black is a pretty forgiving color, especially when you spray it on extra thick. I'm thinking, worst case, maybe I'll have to knock fifty bucks off the price. But then I see a few stray specks of red paint on the engine case.

"Oh, man," I say.

I stop pushing and kneel down to see if I can scrape the specks off with my fingernail. I'm stopped along the side of the road, but really I've reached the end of it. The end of the road, and the end of the Road Rokkit. It's a problem that no amount of fresh paint is going to solve. I see it now. There's a crack running down the outside of the crankcase. It looks like a lightning bolt, and that's what it feels like I've been hit by. It's as long and thin as a strand of hair. It's not thick, but I've learned a few things about engines now. I think of all the vibrations, all the horsepower. This crack will get a little bigger every single time someone rides this bike.

I drop my head into my hands, burying my forehead in both palms.

I can't sell the bike like this.

And where would I get a new crankcase for a vintage Road Rokkit? In the next hour?

I hear a low groan slip through my lips. I can't believe this is how it ends. I know it's just a crack in a piece of metal, but it feels like a wound in a living thing. After all the things I've done, all the problems I've overcome, this just feels like one thing too many. This last little break is the thing that breaks me. I wheel the bike the rest of the way home, cold and stunned and numb.

This crack wasn't there when I took the engine apart, so this happened after that.

That means the carb wasn't the only thing that broke in that crash.

I hate Landrover so much right now. I remember him driving away on his perfect mini-four-wheeler. It seems so unfair, and it makes me so mad. Hatred, anger, a few tons' worth of feeling sorry for myself . . . It's an ugly mix, but at least it keeps me from crying again. I'm so red-hot right now that it's like it boils the tears away. And that's good, because I don't want to be crying when I tell Gene that the stupid deal is off.

Once I get home, I give myself a few minutes to try to get a grip, and then I make the call. "That's too bad" is all he says. What does he care? He's got money. He'll buy something else. But me? All I've got is a cracked bike under a tarp out back and a burning hole in the rent box where it came from.

I go to my room and lie down in the weak gray light coming in through the window. I look over at the clock and watch the numbers crawl forward. It reaches 3:59, and I watch Dad's bet expire. Four o'clock, 4:01. I look out the window and see a few stray snowflakes drift by. St. Patrick's Day or Christmas: Around here, who can tell?

BOXES

I'M STILL LYING on my bed when Dad comes home. It's a loser family reunion. He slams the door so hard behind him that it rattles my window. I head out into the living room, but he's not there. Instead, I see three cardboard boxes scattered on the floor by the door like giant dice. They're all a little beat up. My heart stops. I remember this.

When we moved out of our house, he did the same thing. He refused to pay for new boxes. "Why should I when stores all over town are just throwing them out every day?"

I find him in the kitchen eating St. Patrick's Day cupcakes straight from the box. He finishes one, popping one last bit of yellow cake and green frosting into his mouth. He reaches for another. There are crumbs in his beard, crumbs on the table. "Want one?" he says, slurring the words as he chews.

I shake my head. "What's with the boxes?" I demand, even

though I already know. I just want to hear him say it. I want to hear him admit that he messed up as much as I did

He whips his hand back and throws the cupcake against the wall. It bounces off and leaves a stain that looks like a bright green bullet wound. I flinch a little, but I don't back down. I live here too—and at least I've been trying. "Are we moving again?" I keep my voice steady. I'm to blame too. I know I lost money and that I'll have to tell him now. But I want him to go first. He started this whole mess.

He finally looks at me. "We're short on the rent," he says flatly. "We're going to have to find a new place."

I know I should act surprised, but I don't have the energy. I look at the stain on the wall—shamrock green—the luck of the Irish. I'm sick of pretending.

"You made a bet," I say.

He looks at me closely. Maybe he's trying to figure out what I know or how I know it. Maybe he doesn't even care.

"Bingo!" he says, pointing a finger at my chest.

He doesn't understand. He thinks I guessed.

"You didn't pay the rent last month either," I say.

Dad smiles. "Sure I did," he says. "Straight to the Stubbs brothers."

He reaches for another cupcake, shaking his head. "Doesn't matter anyway. Mr. K's wanted me out of here almost since we moved in. He was always going to get his way, just a matter of time." I'm amazed: He still can't admit this is his fault.

"Dad, I did something—" I begin, but he cuts me off.

"Lots of people bet on it!"

"On the tower," I say, still edging toward admitting what I did.

"Yeah," he says, "on the tower, on St. Paddy's Day."

He's finally admitted it, but it's still not enough for me. My next words slip out of an ugly place inside me. "But they didn't bet the *rent*."

We stare at each other for a few moments and then he looks back down at the box of cupcakes. "Probably not," he admits, his voice softening. I thought I wanted this, but now I realize that there's nothing worse than watching my dad give up. He looks over at the stain on the wall. "I'll clean that up."

Dad gets up to put the box of cupcakes away.

"It wasn't supposed to be this cold," he says, looking like he's talking to the cupcakes. "I wasn't just counting on four-leaf clovers and St. Paddy's. There was the long-range weather forecast too. It wasn't even that bad a winter!"

"I know," I say. "I saw *The Farmer's Year Booke*. This whole stretch was supposed to be warm."

Dad finally looks at me again. He's wearing that same lopsided smile. "See," he says, so quietly that I barely hear it.

I decide to give him something. To stick together. Even though everything is falling apart. "I bought a ticket for tonight too," I say.

"Really?" he says, doubtful.

"Yeah," I say. "Nine p.m."

He makes a stink face. "Bad bet," he says, but look who's talking.

"It would be so great if that tower fell for us."

"It's been so cold," he says. "Lightning would have to strike it."

I nod, and that's when I get the idea.

He's right. Lightning would have to strike that tower for it to fall tonight.

Or something would.

THIN ICE

I WAIT TILL EIGHT O'CLOCK. *This plan will work*, I tell myself. This won't be another number that floats by. I look at Dad, lying on the couch with his face blue from the TV screen. "I'm going for a walk," I say.

I get my parka and grab my old backpack. I'm trying to act normal and look the same as always. I'm already walking out of the room when Dad finally speaks. "We would've been so set," he says. I can tell he's been thinking about it all night.

I don't even know how to feel about that. Should I be mad that he's still clinging to that bet, or sad that it didn't work out? Mostly what I feel is desperate.

It's dark outside. I breathe out and watch my breath float away, and then I zip my parka all the way up. A few days ago, I was all aboard for Building a Better Norton. But right now, I hate this town. I hate how poor it is and how desperate it makes people. I hate that it has people like the Stubbs brothers who'll take your rent. I hate that it has people like my dad who'll just hand it over.

I look back at our place as I reach the edge of the yard. I can see the light on in the little kitchen, the TV filling the living room with shifting colors. I hated this place when we moved in, just because it wasn't the house where I'd grown up. But I realize now how much I'd miss it. I think about that as I walk. It keeps me going.

I keep my hood down on the walk, shielding my face from any headlights. After a few blocks, I can feel my mind downshift. The cool air, the stars, the quiet . . . It calms me down and helps me think. Inside, I could barely wait till eight to leave, but now I realize I'm going to be too early. I can't just hang out there. Someone could see me.

I have my backpack on, so I figure I can kill time in the usual way. It could even be an alibi. So I take all the familiar turns, and pretty soon, I'm bent over and foraging through the trash behind Royston's.

I end up with around a dozen, half cans and half bottles, including two big two-liter ones. Sometimes I leave those—too bulky and the nickel's not worth it—but I've got the space in my pack tonight.

I take the same route to the pond that I took with Dad. The stores are mostly closed now. I don't see anyone out walking.

I don't usually wear my old watch—it's digital with a little light button you can press. It's basically a kid's toy, but I dug it out for tonight. I check it now as I pass beneath the "Thin Ice Days" banner at the entrance to the park. I've got just enough time to scope things out.

It seems a little scarier out here tonight. No people, not much moon, and then there's what I'm planning to do . . . Just thinking about it, my heart begins to hammer in my chest, in my ears. My mouth goes dry. Fear is starting to take over. It's squeezing me like a giant hand, but I can't let it stop me. I check my watch. It's 8:52 p.m. I force myself to breathe: in one, two, out one, two.

And then I go. If I wait any longer, I won't do it.

I start walking toward the edge of the pond. I move my feet mechanically: right-left, right-left. My boots crunch through what's left of the thin, crusty snow. Just ahead of me I see the point where the land ends and the ice begins. The ice glows faintly in the moonlight.

I hold my breath and cautiously step out onto it with my right boot. The ice holds. I step with the left. I am standing on the ice, just a few inches from shore. I look out across it toward the tower. I swear to God it looks one million miles away. It is going to take so many of these short steps to get there, and after killing all that time now I'm afraid I won't have enough left. The time slots for the tickets are every fifteen minutes during prime ice-melting time, but you can't go over. After nine, someone else wins. Stupid.

I slide my right foot forward, breathe, and then slide my left foot out to join it. That's when I hear it. In the stillness between two gusts of wind, I hear a crackling pop so small it could have come from a cereal bowl. It came from the ice. I stop cold.

I look down at my boots: black slabs against the frosty white. They already look like holes in the ice. It feels like a sign, like a premonition of death.

What am I doing? The thought slaps me across the stupid face. I planned to tip the tower a little before nine and win my bet, win the money. It was a cheater's plan, a gambler's plan, but I was desperate.

I knew it was dangerous, but it's one thing to come up with a last-chance idea standing there in the kitchen. It's another on the ice. I could die out here—and for what? Some rent money. Is that what my life is worth?

I remember looking at that betting slip and thinking: *How could he bet so much?*

But now I am betting so much more. I'm betting everything.

And I hate betting!

I'm not willing to lose it all.

I turn and in two quick, get-me-out-of-here steps I'm back on shore. I'm bent over and breathing hard.

Another number floats by as I catch my breath: nine p.m.

I guess that's it, then. I straighten up and begin walking home. But I don't make it more than two steps this time either.

I hear something behind me and turn back again. At first, it's just a shadow in the moonlight, a shape. Then I realize what I'm looking at. Someone is sliding out onto the ice from the other side. They're wearing sneakers, and I can't tell if it's a kid or an adult, and that's when I realize: It's Landrover.

I don't have to wonder what he's doing. I look down at my old watch. The big jerk must have the ticket after mine!

Seeing him out there—out there where I planned to go—gives me the distance to see just how reckless this is. The ice is glowing ghostly in the moonlight. It wasn't that many days ago that we were all expecting it to break up on its own. Yeah, it's been cold this week, but it was warm before that and it's still mid-March. It's a suicide mission.

I am obviously not Landrover's biggest fan, but I was just out there. I know what it's like to be out on that ice with your heart hammering and the wind whipping. I feel this weird connection to him. "No no no," I say, but my voice is soft and low and a gust of wind carries it away.

I force myself to take a deep breath and then shout: "Landrover! Get off the ice!"

I see him flinch, his whole body tensing. He freezes mid-step. I know he heard me, but he doesn't look over. A second later, he pushes his foot the rest of the way forward. Then he slides the other one past it. He isn't stopping.

"Dude!" I call again. "What are you doing?"

He freezes again. Finally, he looks over at me. I see his face, his eyes wide and his expression serious. He raises one hand to his lips, index finger up.

"SHHHHHH!" he hisses as loud as he can.

I look from him to the tower, from the tower to the rope, and from the rope to the clock back on land. He doesn't want anyone to know that he's trying to sink the tower. Forget that. If he won't make noise, I will. "It's not worth it!" I shout.

He looks at me for one more long moment. "You don't know," he says.

I do. But watching someone else do this, it seems so clear. He is going to die out there. Even if the ice doesn't give out under him on its own, he is literally going out there to break it. It's not something you can do halfway—at least not at his size. I have to try again. "Come back," I say. "I have a better idea."

I don't. It's a bluff, and he ignores it. He keeps sliding along the ice. I look over at the clock again: 9:10. His ticket has got to be for 9:15. He's got five minutes, but he's almost to the tower now. He takes a bundle out from inside his coat and unwraps what looks like an old-fashioned hand drill. I've got a jumbo-sized serrated kitchen knife wrapped up in my pack, but I have to admit, that's better.

"Don't!" I hiss, but he does. He kneels down next to the nearest wooden leg of the tower. I see him place the drill point against the ice. All his weight is pressed into the ice right next to the tower's weight—and that's where he's punching through.

My feet are carrying me back toward the edge of the pond now. "Don't! Dude!"

He begins to crank away with the drill anyway. It's 9:13. We're both getting desperate.

"You don't need the money!" I call.

"What do you know?" he says. I'm shouting but he still won't go any louder than you would talk in homeroom.

"You've got a four-wheeler!" I say. In my mind, that shiny blue machine has become a symbol of how much better his life is.

"You dummy!" he says, finally raising his voice. "That's not mine. Someone brought it into the shop for Dad to fix. I just borrowed it, but the engine was worse than they said. I totally fried it chasing after you. It's toast. Dad's gonna *kill* me!"

So much for symbols, I think, because his life is starting to sound awfully familiar.

As soon as he stops talking, I hear a thin, brittle noise. I almost wonder if it's the vibrations from that deep voice of his that make the difference. There's a pop as the drill punches through the ice, then a louder snap, like someone stepping on a twig. The brittle noise becomes a slow crackling.

Landrover's eyes are wide open with fear or surprise or both, the whites glowing in the moonlight as he drops the metal drill, stands, and turns back toward shore. He's finally coming back. I hope it's not too late. He slides his right foot forward urgently, then slides his left foot past it. "That's it," I say. "Keep going. Nice and easy."

The crackle grows, deepens.

He pushes his right foot forward again. Behind him, the leg of the tower finally punches through the ice with a sudden loud pop. The tower tips a few degrees to the side, and the hand drill slides into the hole and silently sinks. Landrover shoots a quick look back over his shoulder.

He disappears through the ice.

It happens so suddenly that I almost doubt my eyes. He's just gone. I stare at the spot where he was and see the small, dark hole that took him down. I look down and see the ice stretching out in front of me. Adrenaline is flooding my system.

Landrover pops to the surface, sputtering water and gasping. He flails at the edge of the ice like he's swimming the crawl. His wet hands smack down, but he can't get a grip. His hands claw and slide, slide and claw. He's scared, desperate.

There's no one out here, no one else in the park on a cold night. The only sounds are the crackling of the ice and the splashing and slapping of the boy about to slip under again.

I take a deep breath and push my right foot forward—back out onto the ice. My boot slides easily across the slick surface. My left foot slides just as easily out to join the right. It's like the ice still wants me here, like it missed me.

I look out toward Landrover, his lips pressed firmly together just above the icy water. Hypothermia will set in soon. I know that from my dad's Alaska shows. I'm wearing heavy boots and a parka. If the ice breaks under me, I won't be able to swim.

I try not to think about it. I concentrate on sliding smoothly. I'm not even halfway there, and I can already feel the thin ice beginning to crackle under my feet.

A larger movement draws my eyes back to the center of the pond. Behind Landrover, the heavy tower is sliding sideways and down. It's following that first leg slowly into the water. I hear a sudden twang, like a guitar string breaking, and see the rope snap free from the clock.

Even now my eyes dart over to the big clock: 9:16.

He didn't win either.

Landrover's face is slick with water and contorted with fear. His numb hands are pawing uselessly at the edge of the ice, breaking it into chunks.

I take one more breath and head out to join him.

I can't believe I'm doing this for *Landrover*, but at this moment, he could be anyone. His terrified eyes, his slipping hands. He could be me. Desperate. He could be Dad.

I slide my right foot forward and then my left. The ice splinters slowly. All around my feet, spiderweb cracks radiate outward.

But the ice doesn't break.

Not yet.

TAKING THE PLUNGE

MY DAD HAS A FEW seasons of a TV show called *Ice Road Truckers* on DVD. It's a show about truck drivers in super-cold, remote parts of Canada. The only way to get stuff from place to place in the winter is to drive big trucks over frozen roads. The most dramatic parts are always when they have to drive over frozen lakes. The trucks go really slow and the ice is really thick, so everything usually looks fine up top. But then they put a camera under the ice.

The ice is always cracking. You can see it and hear it. But all that cracking is just the ice flexing to take the weight. It's the only way the ice can bend. The trucks always seem to make it.

So that's what I'm telling myself now: The ice below me isn't breaking; it's *bending*. I'm getting close to Landrover, and his eyes are locked on me. His hands are on the edge of the ice, but they're not doing anything but shaking. He's not going to last much longer.

His lips are clamped shut right at the water line but they pop open for a quick gulp of air, like a goldfish's. The ice under me groans. *Bending*, I pray. I freeze up. I know I shouldn't be staying still for this long, but the ice around him is riddled with deeper cracks.

"Hold on, dude," I say, my voice shaking with what I pretend is cold.

His eyes are still laser-locked on mine, and I think I see him nod. Very slowly, I begin lowering myself down onto one knee. I don't feel the scrapes or bruises on my leg or side at all now. My backpack shifts on my shoulders, the cans and bottles clinking. I forgot I even had it on, but I have no time to deal with it now. I just leave it.

I'm going to have to lie down, to spread out my weight and reach for him. A little layer of pond water has sloshed up through the broken ice. As soon as my knee touches down, the water soaks through my jeans. It's so cold that I gasp. The shock is almost electric.

Electric . . . like the clock on the shore. And the clock on the shore makes me think of—

"The rope!" I say.

Landrover's eyes get even wider, which I didn't think was possible. Now he is definitely nodding. He's still got some strength left. That's good. I cast my eyes around the gleaming ice until I spot the rope. It looks like a snake, lying in a long lazy S-shape alongside the tower.

"Hold on," I say. I begin to stand up, but I move too fast. I put too much weight on too small a spot. There's a quick pop as my right boot punches through the ice.

My whole body follows, and I plunge straight through into the icy water.

The shock of the cold is overwhelming. I close my eyes, clench my lips, and hold my breath as my head disappears below the surface. The water is dark and so cold it burns. I can feel my parka filling up and my boots dragging me down. I wonder how far I'll sink—maybe all the way to the bottom. But almost immediately, I feel myself pulled back up toward the surface.

Landrover? I think, but it's not him.

It's my backpack. I realize there's air trapped inside the cans and bottles I collected, and it's lifting me up. I know I don't have much time. With the strap of my backpack tugged tight under my right arm, I reach down and claw at the laces of my boots. I sink down lower, dragging the backpack down with me. My fingers are too numb for me to know for sure, but I think I've torn the loops open. I kick wildly. The boots come off and suddenly I'm lighter.

Now I reach over with my left arm and pull the backpack around in front of me. I thrust my left arm through the other strap and suddenly I am wearing my backpack in front. It begins to lift me up. I need air. I turn my head toward the gap in the ice above me and kick.

I break the surface. I blow water out my nose and suck in a breath. I look around, cold water running down my face and into my eyes. The wounded ice has given out. The tower has collapsed onto its side behind Landrover and is bobbing lazily in the water. There is no longer solid ice between us, just jagged floating chunks. I begin to swim in his direction in an awkward doggy paddle. The backpack is almost like a boogie board underneath me.

I have to push through the jagged ice with my chin. I'm probably cutting myself but I'm too frozen and numb to feel a thing.

Water must be getting in through the nylon of my pack by now, in through the zipper. Soon it will begin to fill the cans and bottles.

I reach Landrover but don't stop. I need to get to the rope. If I can reach the edge of the ice behind him, I think I can grab it. I try to swim past him, but he isn't having it. As soon as I'm in range, he lurches out and grabs at me with his frozen claw hands.

"Ow!" I sputter as one of his hands slaps down on my head and tugs hard on my hair. His other hand is up high on my arm now and he's dragging me closer. His hand slips down to the strap of my backpack and I begin to panic.

At first, I try to fight him off. It's impossible. He's huge and strong and all clawing hands and desperation. He's going to kill us both. I can't get enough breath to explain that I'm going for the rope.

I get a better idea.

"Come on," I gasp, grabbing him by the shoulders and turning.

Soon, we're both on our sides, heads barely above water and the backpack sandwiched between us. I begin to kick and, without either of us saying a word about it, he does too.

We swim for the edge. Slowly. So slowly.

We sink as we go, the backpack and bottles filling. I'm not sure we're going to make it. I'm dog tired and chilled to the bone. But I keep going. I want to live. I want to save Landrover—even if it's just to see the look on his face when he realizes he owes me.

So I kick once more, twice, and the top of my head hits the edge of the ice. I twist around, and there it is: the rope. I throw my right hand over my head, and it smacks down on the ice. I flop it around but I have to watch to see when it reaches the rope because I have no feeling in my fingers.

My hand falls on the rope. But my hand won't work. I can't make it grab hold. Desperate, I turn my arm from the shoulder. My half-closed hand slides underneath the rope. My system shutting down, the last of my adrenaline burning away, I start twirling my arm. The rope wraps around it like spaghetti around a fork.

I tug hard, bending my arm at the elbow. I do it again. My vision bounces as my face slides over the edge of the ice. I throw my other arm at the rope. My fingers frozen stiff, I hook in. I pull hard. My shoulder slides up and over the edge of the ice. And not just mine. Landrover is latched on, his arms hooked under my armpits, frozen there.

I pull again. And again. I go until I have no strength left.

The two of us are lying on our sides, facing each other in a puddle of icy water. Behind us, the ice is a fractured mess. In front of us, it's a solid sheet heading toward shore.

My teeth are chattering hard, but I manage to say a few words. "We're gonna have to slide."

I don't think Landrover hears me, but when I start inchworming along, he starts inchworming too. We bring our knees up until they're touching, then we straighten our legs out as we push forward.

We make it to shore that way. We're out of the water but still wet. I am way past exhausted. I want to just lie here and rest, maybe even sleep, but I know I'll die if I do.

"We have to get up." At first I think the words are in my head, but then Landrover says it again, louder: "Eakins, we have to get up!"

And then, amazingly, he does. I'd always heard that this guy was an amazing athlete, tough as nails, pure muscle—all those things people say about middle school superstars. But it's something else to see it for myself. Landrover makes this face— just pure effort and pain. His stiff arms push down, his rigid legs begin to bend. "AAAAAAAH!" he yells, and just like that, he's standing.

I have no idea how he did it, where he found the strength. But the next thing he does is just as surprising. He reaches one frozen hand down for me.

36

UBER COOL

"GET THAT JACKET OFF!" barks Landrover.

"What?"

"It's soaking. Get it off."

I know he's right, but I can barely even stand. I'm swaying on my feet, dripping icy water onto the frozen ground. I see him standing there doing the same. He's visibly shivering and pawing at the front of his jacket with his frozen hands, unable to grasp the zipper. He turns, gets right in my face, and yells: "Now!"

Even shaking like a cell phone set on vibrate, he's a big scary dude, so I try. I shrug my backpack off my front and it hits the ground with a wet thud. I stick my frozen hand into the neck of my jacket and push the zipper all the way down.

My parka slips to the ground like a wet seal. The cold wind hits my soaked shirt. *How is this better?* I look over at Landrover, and he has his jacket off too. He probably just tore it off like the Hulk.

"Push-ups!" he shouts.

He has lost his mind. His brain must have frozen solid.

But he shouts, "Now!" in my face again. Next thing I know, we're both back down on the ground and cranking out push-ups on frozen hands. I get like two and a half in before I have to resort to half push-ups on my knees. Next to me, Landrover is cranking out perfect push-ups at a machinelike pace.

He's counting softly: ". . . seven, eight, nine." When he gets to ten he starts over at one. If I could do that many, I'd definitely keep track. But he's not trying to set a record. He's trying to survive, and watching him, I can see the genius of it. As he cranks away, I see the color return to his face. His arms too.

He pops up. Still cranking out half push-ups from my knees, I see him shake his whole body out like a wet dog. Then he shakes out his hands and flexes them. His blood is pumping now. And I can feel it: Mine is too! I stand up and start doing jumping jacks. "Get it, dawg!" he says, reaching down for something in his coat pocket.

I'm breathing hard now. It's working. The feeling is starting to come back into my arms and legs. That's good—but it feels *so bad*! A thousand painful pinpricks fire under my skin. My body is working again, and it hurts—but it sure beats the alternative.

I do one more jumping jack and then bend over, sucking cold air into greedy lungs. I look over and see Landrover taking a cell phone out of a ziplock bag.

"You knew you'd fall in," I say, my voice a breathy croak.

"Nah," he says. "But I considered the possibility."

An amazing thing happens. Still dripping wet, exhausted, and with just enough feeling in my body to realize how freaking cold it is, I laugh. Like really laugh. "What are you doing?" I say, watching him press his cold fingers hard onto the touch screen.

"Using Uber," he says. "I'm allowed. For emergencies."

"Yeah," I say, picking a tiny, perfect icicle off my hair with shivering fingers. "I think this qualifies."

It's my first Uber ride, but for the first fifteen minutes or so, we don't go anywhere. We just sit in the back of the black sedan by the entrance to the park, drying off and warming up. I'll give the driver credit. He doesn't hesitate to let two soaking kids into his nice car. He just takes one look at our shivering, purple-lipped faces and cranks the heat up all the way.

We talk for some of those fifteen minutes. We swear the driver guy to secrecy first, but he honestly doesn't seem to care about anything other than us warming up enough to get out of his car. I tell Landrover everything. Well, almost everything. I don't tell him where I got the money for the bike, just that I couldn't afford to lose it. I tell him all the rest: about the bad paint job and broken crankcase and even the late shift.

Maybe I'm saying too much, I think. But honestly, it feels good to tell someone, especially someone who knows what a flywheel is.

"Wh-what are you g-going to tell your dad?" I say once I finish up my side of the story. I'm warmer now, but I still can't shake the shivering.

"I'm gonna tell him what happened," Landrover says with a shrug. "I don't have the money for that new engine now anyway."

"Is he r-really gonna k-kill you?" I say.

He shrugs. "I've already survived one near-death experience tonight. And how much more trouble can I really get into? I'm already maxed out. I might even confess to a few other things while I'm at it."

"G-genius," I say.

The car lets me off first, right outside the house. I walk across the yard in dirty, wet socks. My boots are at the bottom of the pond. I am carrying my wet parka like a drowned animal.

I'm just gonna tell him what happened, I think as I open the door.

But he's asleep on the couch, so I tiptoe to my room instead. I peel off my clothes and get All The Blankets. Later, after I hear him go into his room, I head out and take a bath so long and hot that it makes me miss Mr. Bubble.

I almost died tonight. Instead, I saved a life. I set out to do a bad thing, but I did a good one. And no one knows about any of that. No one except Landrover, who didn't even say thank you, and a lifesaving Uber driver who is sworn to secrecy.

OPEN UP

I SLEEP IN ON SATURDAY. A juicy steak like me is just going to take a little longer to defrost, you know? But seriously, I look like death in the bathroom mirror. My lips are still a little blue and my chin is cut up from the ice.

Dad isn't around to see this sorry sight. I find his note when I finally make it to the kitchen: "Looking at places today. Food in fridge." I check the fridge. I'm pretty sure he's talking about the last two cupcakes. Back in the living room, I see more boxes by the door.

I collapse onto the couch under two blankets and a bad-mood funk a mile deep.

Things suck infinitely right now. Where do I even start?

We're moving out, and who knows where we'll end up. Could be a smaller apartment, a broken-down place on the edge of town, one of those dicey motels out by the freeway . . . Even if I'm not going to be homeless, I'm still losing my home.

I stole money from Dad. That money could be the difference between a decent apartment and a roach-infested motel room. And that money's not coming back, because I poured it into a bike that's currently lying on its side in the lawn mower shed.

And I haven't even told him yet. That's not going to be pretty, but I have to. He needs to know how much he has to spend. Speaking of which . . .

He's gambling again. I'm not the only one who messed up here.

The contest is over this weekend, which means so is the late shift. I'll miss it.

And finally, I still feel as cold and clammy as a frozen turkey.

So that's where my head's at—up my butt, basically—when I hear a knock at the door mid-morning. *What now?* I think. But the knocking continues, so I finally throw back the blanket and get up. "Coming!" I shout.

Stupid, I think. Now they know I'm here.

"Yeah?" I say at the door.

"Open up."

The voice is muffled by the door but vaguely familiar. I open up. It's Landrover.

He's dressed in a different coat from last night, and he has a big ugly bruise on the side of his face. It could be from out on the ice, but I don't think so.

"Dad's gonna kill me!" he said last night, and it looks like his dad gave it a try.

"Uh, hey?" I say. I am standing there in red-and-white pajamas and a fuzzy green sweater, both a few sizes too large to accommodate the way I'm made. I must look like a Christmas ornament.

"Where's the bike?" says Landrover, swinging an overstuffed pack off his back and onto the floor. It clanks when it hits. I don't know why he's here. I'm honestly a little too surprised to form a coherent thought at the moment. But after what the two of us went through together last night, I'm willing to give him the benefit of the doubt one more time.

"I'll show you," I say. "Just let me put on like eighty-seven layers first."

He waits on the couch while I bundle up. I know his place must be way nicer than this, but I'm not embarrassed. I feel lucky to still be here, even if it's just through the weekend. "Okay," I say, emerging so bundled up in layers that I look like that kid in *A Christmas Story* who can't move his arms.

"What's in there, anyway?" I say, nodding at the backpack as we head down the stairs.

"Some tools, J-B Weld, paint thinner," he starts. "The usual."

I snort out a laugh. I'm not sure what good any of this will do, but at least I know why he's here now—and it's not like I've got anything else going on.

The cold is waiting for me outside like an old enemy. Even as bundled up as I am, I start shivering again. "I'm not sure we should be out here right now," I say. Landrover's lips were so purple last night Esme would have been jealous.

"Your mom's gone and your dad's not home, right?" he says. The words hit me hard. Sometimes I hate living in a small town.

"Yeah," I admit.

"So what's the problem?"

"I meant the cold."

"I know you did," he says with a little smirk. "Here, take this."

He tosses me something from his coat pocket. I catch it and feel the warmth right through my gloves. It's an electric pocket warmer. "I use them for ice fishing," he says.

I unzip my coat and put it in the inside pocket, up against my ribs. It feels good. I fished him out of the ice last night, but I don't think he needs me to remind him of that.

I duck into the shed and throw the tarp off the bike. "Here it is," I say, wheeling it backward into view.

He looks at it for a few seconds, sizing it up.

"Okay, let's get started," he says. "We don't want to be out here all day."

He's here to pay me back for ice-fishing him out. I appreciate it, but it's cold out, even with the pocket warmer, and I'm not sure I see the point. "Why?"

"So you can sell it, dipstick."

"I already told the guy the deal's off. He's probably bought a Honda by now!"

Landrover looks down. "Oh, yeah," he says. "I guess that's it, then."

"I guess so." I feel the last little bit of hope drain out of me like a limp balloon.

He slaps the arm of my jacket, smiling. "You big dummy!" he says. "This thing's a Road Rokkit. People kill for these."

"What people?" I say.

"Dude, seriously? Do you even remember where I work? I listed it this morning on one of the private collector sites. Got three offers in like an hour."

I feel a little bit of hope return, like a single sunbeam breaking through the clouds. "But the engine is cracked."

Landrover is kneeling by the bike now. "Engine's not cracked. The case is."

"What's the difference?"

"BIG difference," he says. "The case is an easy fix."

And just like that, I feel the sun shine in. Hope. The bike is fixable—it's easy, even! This isn't over.

"You're really good at this, huh?" I say.

"Grew up in an auto parts store," he says. "It's not as great as it sounds."

I'm standing above him, holding the bike by the handlebars. The bruise on the side of his face is black and purple and even a little brown. "I guess you'd know."

He swings his pack onto the ground again. "I'm going to take this cover off, and when I do, you start stripping the paint." He reaches inside his pack and hands me a can of paint remover and a brush.

"Wait till I get the cover off," he adds. "I do *not* want that stuff in my hair."

He gets the crankcase off fast, then shifts over to the side and gets to work fixing it. I start carefully brushing on the paint remover. This stuff smells like death. He takes out some kind of small hand tool from his pack and starts grinding away. I think it's a Dremel like Dad used to have.

"How much did all this cost?" I say over the low hum. I made a solemn vow while I was lying awake last night: I'm back on bottle-and-can money. No more rent-box raids.

"I didn't necessarily pay for it," says Landrover with a smile.

"What if your dad finds out?"

He looks up at me. He's still smiling, but it's a different kind of smile now. "Let's just say he's not exactly going to call the cops on me at the moment."

"Right," I say. Not until that bruise fades, anyway.

"My dad gambles," I blurt out. I don't know why. Or I guess maybe I do.

"My mom's gone too," he replies.

For a while we just work. The paint on the bike is starting to bubble up right before my eyes. The image I had in my head of Landrover's perfect life is bubbling up and peeling away too.

"It's this town," Landrover says after a while. "It takes a toll, you know?"

I do, but I've already said as much as I'm ready to about that. Instead I say: "Aren't you trying to build a better one? For the contest, I mean."

He laughs. "Kind of. I guess. I'm building, like, a Transformer. You know what that is? It's a model of the factory and it transforms into a robot. It's pretty sweet. The eyes light up red and I'm trying to get it to walk."

"What if there are people inside when it transforms?" I say, thinking about my dad.

"They can go along for the ride," he says. "More fun than making shoes."

"Definitely," I say, but I still don't understand how that makes the town better. "You're never gonna win with that."

He laughs again. "I know that. It's just cool. And anyway, your friend's going to win."

"Nephi?"

"Yeah."

"You really think so?"

"Yeah, he's totally gonna win," he says.

But that's not what I meant. I was asking about the friend part.

We're both freezing, so we go inside while we're waiting for the paint thinner to work its dark magic so we can repaint. Landrover wants to apply the J-B Weld to the crankcase inside anyway, so it will dry better. It's like a heavy-duty epoxy.

"This place is really clean," he says, looking around my room. "Your dad make you clean?"

I look down at my carefully made bed. The embarrassing thing is, he doesn't. "Mmm," I say, noncommittal.

He spreads a small plastic sheet out on my floor, sits down next to it, and begins mixing the epoxy.

"Is that stuff strong enough?"

"Totally. The metal will break before this stuff does. And a crack this thin, you'll hardly be able to see it."

"So, three offers already?" I say. I don't want to bother him while he's working, but I really want to know how much we're talking.

"Could be more by now," he says, not even looking up. "But this bike, this condition, you're not going to get more than six hundred."

"Fine with me," I say. Six hundred is what I was hoping for! With Dad's paycheck and what we have left, it's enough. My next question is a little more complicated, but I really want to know this too. "Why'd you hate me so much?"

He turns his face halfway toward me and then stops and looks back down at his work. He starts slowly applying the J-B Weld. "Yeah, I've been thinking about that," he says. "Just since last night, you know?"

"I figured."

"It's hard to explain. It's just . . . school can be so cool sometimes."

I stare at him, incredulous. "Maybe for you."

"Okay, fair. But it's the only place I really like anymore, and I get that it's maybe harder for you . . ."

Maybe???

"But then it's like you ruin it for the rest of us too, moping around all alone like a freak." He pauses. "Sorry," he adds. "About the freak part."

I shrug. "So it wasn't about me being friends with Maps?"

"Maybe a little."

"And it wasn't about—"

"Look," he says, before he even hears what I was going to say. "I don't know why. I just have a lot of anger right now, all right? And I don't have anywhere else to put it."

I just look at him. He's talking about anger like it's a bag of groceries. I'm going to have to think about that some more, but I know he just admitted something. I know it probably wasn't easy. "Sometimes I just pull inside myself," I say, "like a turtle."

"Everyone does that," he says.

"Yeah, but for me it can last years."

He nods. "Same with the anger."

He just works for a while after that, and I just shut up and let him. "One of the guys interested in the bike is local," he says after a few minutes. "We're meeting him tomorrow morning."

We? I look at Landrover one more time. The words are on the tip of my tongue: *You're all right.* But I don't say them. I can't quite get there, not yet. I know more about him now, more about his life. But I'm not an idiot. I still remember how he treats kids who didn't just save his life. So instead I just say, "Thanks."

WHAT ELSE IS THERE?

"HEY, DAD. I need to tell you something, and the only thing I'm going to ask is that, whatever you're gonna do, you wait until after I finish talking to do it."

He looks up at me from the couch. I sit in the chair.

"What's on your mind?" he says

"What isn't?" I say.

He cracks a smile, and that's when I strike. "I took some money from the rent box!"

Dad sits up fast. "You did *what*? How much? You better still have that money!"

"I don't."

He swings his legs over the side of the couch.

"I'm not done talking yet! Please!" He starts to stand. "You took money too! For your bet!"

He stops, sinks back a little. He's poised right on the edge of the couch now.

"It's my money, Ked."

"It's our money, Dad."

He looks at the ceiling. His fists are balled up, but I can see his lips moving as he counts to three. It's a thing he does. Once he's done, he says, "What did you do?"

So I tell him. I tell him how I bought the bike, and how I fixed it up, and I *definitely* tell him that there's a dude who wants to buy it tomorrow morning.

He is staring at me now. He's still angry—*very* angry. I can see his pulse beating in the wormlike vein above his right eye. But I can see that he's thinking about something. "How much you think you'll get?"

"Could be six hundred," I say. "That's like four hundred profit. Almost."

So now he knows how much I took too. He gets that doing-math look.

"That'd be enough," he says, his voice just a little softer.

"Yeah, so the thing is: You can't kill me. You need me to sell the bike to this guy. He's, like, expecting *me*."

Dad sits back, just a little. A smile slides onto his face. "Oh, I can kill you, son," he says. "I just can't kill you *yet*."

I laugh, but it's a nervous laugh.

"Is that what happened to your face?" he says, pointing at the cuts and scrapes. "The bike?"

"Sure," I start, but then I change my mind. There's been too much lying already, too much hiding the truth. This is my dad; he's all I've got left. If I can't trust him, then, well, what exactly

215

do I have? "No. I tried to tip the tower last night. To win my bet. But I fell through the ice. And I lost anyway." I don't tell him about Landrover. That part doesn't feel like it's mine to tell.

"Oh my God," says Dad, sitting up again. "Oh my God . . ."

"If I give you this money, you have to stop gambling," I'm saying. "I'm serious." But then I see his face. He is stunned, straight-up shocked.

"Ked, you could've died," he says. "Are you okay?"

I'd kind of been trying to forget the whole thing. I never thought I'd tell anyone anyway. But now, seeing all the color drain from his face and hearing the little quiver in his voice, it finally hits me just how close I came. I was one shoelace away, one less two-liter bottle . . . My face probably looks like his now. I feel that little hitch in my throat, like I might cry. I need to finish talking before that happens.

"I'm serious," I repeat. "No more gambling."

He looks at me. "I could've killed you."

I don't say anything. He's not the one who made me go there last night.

"I'm done," he says. And it's not so much the words as the way he says them. He's looking me in the eyes. He looks serious, and I really want to believe him. But he's made promises before and it hasn't worked.

"You've got to go back to Our Lady of the Horse Track."

He looks me in the eyes and nods. "And you can't take any-more dumb chances," he says.

"Deal," I say. "Should we, like, shake on it?"

He shakes his head and finally stands up. He waves me up too.

"Aw, Dad," I say, pretending I don't want to do this. But we do. We hug it out. This counts at least as much as a handshake. I feel that little hitch again. My eyes start to water right into Dad's scratchy sweater. I think I might cry again, but this is a different kind of crying, so I go ahead and let myself.

"I'm sorry, Dad," I say.

"I am too," he says.

It feels good to say. It feels good to hear. Neither one of us is pretending to be right, or even less wrong. We're just forgiving each other and promising to do better. And what else even is there?

"I love you, son," I hear.

Oh, yeah. There's that.

LIKE MOOKIE BETTS

THE MAN WHO wants the bike shows up at the Royston's parking lot first thing Sunday morning wearing a faded Red Sox cap. His name is Doug. He's about my dad's age, and he has a belly on him. "That it?" he says, lifting his chin toward the bike.

I look down at the Road Rokkit, shiny and red with its new paint on the first sunny morning in a week. *Does he think I have another one behind my back?* "Yep."

He looks at it carefully, stroking his chin and just generally making a show of sizing it up. "It runs?"

"Like Mookie Betts," says Landrover. I think it's pretty clever to mention a Red Sox player to this guy. He's obviously had that cap since forever. But we've all got our game faces on, so I don't acknowledge it.

"You're the kid from the auto parts store, right?" he says.

Landrover nods.

"Well, I guess you'd know, then."

It didn't occur to me that Landrover would be considered some kind of expert on this. But the way he smiles now makes me think he did. He's confident and in his element, just like at school.

"What happened to your face?" says Doug, looking at the bruise.

"Just naturally handsome," says Landrover.

I look at the bruise too, and a thought finally works its way to the surface. *I should say something, to someone.* This will take more thinking, but I owe him that much.

The negotiation continues. You can just look at Doug and see that he was probably never much of an athlete, never that popular. He's overmatched by Landrover, even at thirteen, and he seems to recognize that now. He turns back to me.

I see his eyes slide to my back for the second or third time. If he asks me what happened to that, I'm going to say the same thing Landrover did. Instead, he fires out a number. "Five hundred bucks."

"Are you kidding?" says Landrover.

"Do you know how many people want this bike?" I say. I begin to turn the handlebars like I'm going to walk the bike right back out of the parking lot.

"Okay, okay, five fifty!"

"Six," I say. I leave off the "hundred" like they do in the movies. I imagine telling Nephi and Esme about this, and it makes me smile a little.

Doug is watching me closely, sizing me up, and I guess that

little smile looks like confidence to him because he nods once and says, "Deal."

Before I can hold out my hand to shake, he raises his and points the index finger toward the sky. "*If* it starts," he says.

It just started fifteen minutes ago, but I'm still nervous as he reaches down for the pull cord. The thin, patched-up crack is almost invisible under the fresh black paint, and Landrover says that sort of repair is just standard for bikes and quads. If Doug sees it, he doesn't say.

"You gotta pull it hard," I say.

"I know," says Doug. "I've mowed a lawn."

He pulls it and it doesn't even sputter this time. Just two quick puffs and it skips straight to *vroom*. I can't help smiling. Landrover fixed the case, but I fixed the engine. It was *in a bag* when I got it.

Doug revs the throttle twice—*vroom vroom!* He's smiling too.

He cuts the engine. Next thing I know, he's counting out the money and placing it in my hand. Six crisp new hundred-dollar bills . . . So awesome.

"Pleasure doing business with you boys," he says.

"Go Sox," says Landrover.

"Go Sox," Doug and I agree.

AND THE WINNERS ARE . . .

BACK AT HOME, I get changed for the contest. It's in the school gym, which is all decorated for the occasion. Dad is in a good mood and he drives me there, even though it's a short walk and finally warm out. We bump into Mr. Feig by the door. He's kind of like the host for this. I introduce him to Dad, and then I thank him. "I appreciate you letting me be there, even though I wasn't, you know, Building a Better Norton."

"To me, watching you guys sitting around and solving problems, thinking about how to make things better, that *is* building a better Norton," he says. He's in a good mood too.

"Or how to get them running again, anyway."

"That too," he says with a chuckle. "See you Monday."

He means in maker space, and I think about that for a second. He made space for us after school. But he barely even tried to keep us in regular maker space. Maybe he thought that was a better solution. Or maybe it was just easier and he's really busy.

I take one last look at Mr. Feig from under my hair as we walk away. He's not perfect, but he's trying. Sounds familiar.

Dad spots some guys from the factory and before I know it they're huddled up and talking over paper cups of coffee. I start scoping out the gym. It's decked out in paper streamers and balloons, and the contest entries are on folding tables in the center. I see Esme first, because she's taller and more purple. Then I spot Nephi. I can't wait to tell them my news, but this is their moment. I see Landrover last. They're all too busy setting up for the judges to notice me. In addition to the kids I recognize from this school, there are some others here too. There's a little group from the Catholic school, and at least one who's homeschooled. It's definitely a community-wide event.

I'm wearing my standard public event outfit: baggy pants and a big white button-up shirt (unbuttoned) over a good T-shirt (the Green Lantern symbol, because GL can make anything).

The bleachers are already filling up, so I look around for an open spot to sit. I see Maps sitting next to Joe. They see me, and Maps waves me over. *Really?* I think.

I point to myself and mouth: "Me?"

"Get up here!" he calls.

I clamber up the steps and slide into their row.

"Hey," I say.

"Hey," they say.

"Aren't you competing?" I ask Joe. "Where's your model?"

"I didn't finish in time," he says. "Lucky thing for them too."

"Yeah, right."

"So why are you guys here?"

"We're rooting for Neff," says Maps.

"Oh! Right!" I say with zero chill. "Me too."

And it's true. I am rooting for Nephi, but not just for him.

The judges go around from table to table. One of them is a college professor from Bowdoin, and one of them is an inventor "As seen on *Shark Tank*!" They have microphones and they ask the contestants questions about their models and how they would make "this great town even better." (The inventor asks that question. I don't think she's from around here.)

The judges reach Esme's table. "It's hard to see from here," I tell the others, "but her model is really good. It's super artistic."

"It's beautiful," the inventor says into her microphone. My head bobs up and down like it's on a spring.

"But who'd want to paint their whole building black?" says the professor. Jerk.

Nephi is next. He and Esme are set up right next to each other. "This is it, boys," says Maps. And I realize something that should have been obvious. Just because he doesn't sit with Nephi at lunch anymore, just because I don't see them hanging out all the time, it doesn't mean they're not still friends. And if that's true of them . . .

"Let's go, Neff!" I shout, loud enough that he looks up. He sees us and smiles, but it's a nervous smile. The judges have just reached his table. He turns on the motor and points to the gauge as the water in the tank begins to churn.

The professor asks him a question about the motor, and when Nephi answers it easily, he ups the stakes. He asks him a complicated question about the math—or maybe it's about measuring the electricity? Honestly, I'm not even sure—it's that complex. But Nephi answers it, and the professor nods his approval. "Oooooh," I hear from the crowd around us.

"Nailed it," says Joe.

The three of us high-five like we had anything to do with that.

The judges move on. The competition is tough.

The judges reach Landrover's table. The crowd cheers as he unfolds his model of the factory into a robot named "NorTron." They cheer even louder when its eyes light up and it takes a few herky-jerky steps. The other two look surprised when I cheer too.

"How would this make this great town even better?" asks the inventor.

"It would make it cooler," says Landrover. The crowd laughs.

In the end, Nephi wins. We all cheer for that. I even hoot and swirl my fist in the air. The crowd around us agrees. It's a good call by the judges.

Afterward, we file down out of the bleachers to congratulate Nephi. Esme is already there. "You were robbed," I say because she still looks a little mad.

That lightens her up a little. "I think the judges were paid," she jokes. "Were you?" She means for the bike.

"Yep," I say, my smile getting even wider.

We hear some noise near us and look over. Landrover's got a little crowd around him. He's got the controller in his hand and is making NorTron walk across the gym floor. The bruise has faded a little now, or maybe he's got something on there to cover it up.

"It's better than I thought," admits Esme. I don't answer. I know there's something there that still needs fixing.

Then Esme and I congratulate Nephi. We have to wait in line to do it, so then we bust on him for big-timing us. He is so happy that he can hardly talk, but he still manages to shoot that idea down: "I've always got time for the late shift."

It's a little sad because the late shift is probably over now that the contest is. Nephi seems to read my mind. "Am I going to see you guys in maker space on Monday?" he says. "There will probably be room, now that this is over."

"If you're lucky," says Esme.

They both turn to me. "If you're not," I say.

They think that's pretty funny.

"I used up all my luck today anyway," Nephi says, and Esme agrees.

ONE WEEK LATER

I USED TO THINK my whole life had been stolen, piece by piece, but I figured something out. That's how you put a life back together too. Just little pieces, but they add up.

I say hi to Maps at school now. It's just super normal, like no big deal. Sometimes we even talk, if we have time. I sit with Nephi and Joe at the makers' table at lunch, and I'm with them again in maker space. Most of the makers are working together to build a hydraulic arm that really flexes.

Nephi, Esme, and I have our own project. We're building a pocket bike from scratch. The hardest thing is getting enough used parts. Fortunately, I know a guy at the auto parts store.

Landrover and I aren't friends, exactly. That was probably

never going to happen. But we're even now, and we understand each other a lot better. He's not on my case anymore, and people have noticed. Even Haley and Becca. People kind of take their cues from a guy like that.

He and his dad are getting help too. As far as they know, it was an anonymous tip—just what happens when you show up to a community-wide event with that kind of bruise. Anyway, his dad can afford the family therapy, and honestly, I think they can both use the anger management.

As for my dad, he paid off Mr. K (and he put a lock on the rent box). He even went to his first meeting at Our Lady of the Horse Track. He says the coffee's not as bad as he expected. He's still funny. He's still trying. He's still my dad.

Remember what I was saying before, how no one is just one thing? How people surprise you, like Esme and Nephi and even Landrover have surprised me? Well, I was thinking about that and I decided to take one more shot with someone important to me. "Hey, Danny," I said. "Wait up!"

And in a way, he did surprise me.

He didn't wait.

I'm basically okay with it, though. He was honest, and I tried. I don't know what's going on beneath the surface with him. I just know that something is. He looked back when he was walking away, and I don't know what he saw.

But I know who was standing there. It wasn't just a kid with a rare condition, because I'm more than that one thing too. I'm a maker, a builder, a guy who's braver than he thought, and a guy who smiles more than he used to.

If he saw my back, then that's on him.

That's what I look like.

I'm what I do.

I'm Ked Eakins, and I live in Norton, Maine.

AUTHOR'S NOTE

On Thin Ice is a work of fiction, but it deals with many real-world issues. I'd like to take a moment to address a few of them here.

Kyphosis is a real condition, one that really does sometimes affect kids and teens. Ked's condition is unusual in a number of ways, including its early start and severity. His experience isn't meant to represent anyone else's, and his response to it is not meant to be perfect. It is just one fictional kid's response to a rare condition manifesting itself in a rarer way.

This book was inspired by Victor Hugo's *The Hunchback of Notre-Dame*. Because of that, I included that same back condition that has captured the human imagination for centuries, for better or worse. This time, though, I wanted to keep the portrayal based on reality, rather than on folklore, stories, or movies. Everyone is going through something. Sometimes our challenges are visible, and sometimes they aren't. We all deal with those challenges in our own way.

Just, please, don't steal the rent money.

Other characters are dealing with challenges of their own: Ked's dad has a gambling addiction. It's a big problem, but there are some excellent resources available to help. The National Council on Problem Gambling (ncpgambling.org) runs a 24-hour, confidential helpline at 1-800-522-4700.

And then there's Landrover. Child abuse can happen to anyone—even a big dude like him. If you are not living in a safe situation, or if you witness abuse of a friend or family member, find an adult you trust and tell them what is happening. You can also talk to someone twenty-four hours a day at the Childhelp National Child Abuse Hotline: 1-800-4-A-CHILD (1-800-422-4453).

On a happier note, maker space plays a big role in this book. You can find some great info on starting and improving maker spaces at edutopia.org/article/maker-education-resources. And Edutopia was founded by George Lucas, the guy who created *Star Wars*. Ked would approve!

And finally, no, you can't buy a Road Rokkit. (I wish!) It's a made-up brand based on real minibikes. It runs on the same stuff in the same way, but the bike and Ked's repairs are streamlined and tweaked a bit here and there to fit the story without getting too technical. For example, the bike has a diaphragm carburetor and—never mind. Too technical!

I have been working on this story off and on for six years—building and rebuilding it. That is by far the longest of any of my books. I hope you enjoyed it.

—Michael Northrop

ABOUT THE AUTHOR

Michael Northrop is the *New York Times* bestselling author of the middle-grade adventure series TombQuest, the graphic novel *Dear Justice League*, and other books for kids and teens. His first young adult novel, *Gentlemen*, earned him a Publishers Weekly Flying Start citation, and his second, *Trapped*, was an Indie Next List selection. His first middle-grade novel, *Plunked*, was named one of the best children's books of the year by the New York Public Library and was selected for NPR's Backseat Book Club. He is originally from Salisbury, Connecticut, a small town in the foothills of the Berkshire Mountains, where he mastered the arts of BB-gun shooting, tree climbing, and field-goal kicking with only moderate injuries. After graduating from NYU, he worked at *Sports Illustrated Kids* for twelve years, the last five of those as baseball editor. Visit him online at michaelnorthrop.net.